QUEEN OF FEATHERS

QUEEN OF FEATHERS

MAGIC & MECHANICALS BOOK 7

JESSICA MARTING

SHADOW PRESS

Queen of Feathers (Magic & Mechanicals Book 7)

Copyright © 2025 J.L. Turner

ISBN 978-1-989780-42-8

Cover art by German Creative

Edited by Christine Kirchoff

Unexpected Mate (A Magic & Mechanicals Short Story)

Copyright © 2024, 2025 J.L. Turner

AUTHOR'S NOTE

Even though I'm Canadian, I write fiction in American English despite knowing in my heart that "colour" and "favourite" are correct. You'll notice that I've used the British/Canadian spelling of "gryphon" in *Queen of Feathers* between American colors and favorites because it looks infinitely cooler than "griffin." Indie authors get to decide their own style sheets. Sorry for not being sorry.

And to my fellow Canadians during this time of uncertainty and increasing threats to our sovereignty as this book goes to publication: ELBOWS UP!

CHAPTER 1

London, April 1891

IT WAS funny how Beatrice had never noticed the perpetual smug look on Reginald's face until the evening he waltzed into her private parlor demanding she consent to a divorce. Funny or tragic, depending on how one looked at Beatrice's evidently poor way of reading the husband she had been married to for twenty years.

Nineteen and a half, a small voice reminded her as she scanned the last paragraphs of the settlement. It would have been an even twenty had Reginald held off on divorcing her until October. Instead, he had unilaterally decided their marriage was over ten days after their nineteenth wedding anniversary. The six months since had been spent tersely discussing the terms of their split, which quickly escalated to screaming, insults, and threats on both sides. Only Reginald deserved them. Now, it was coming to an official end in the office belonging to Mr. Simpson, Beatrice's solicitor.

Her hand hovered over the spot where she should sign,

the silver pen heavy in her fingers. Reginald's signature had been inked above the spot where she was to write her name, his barely legible black loops were still wet. A petty part of her wanted to smear the ink, but she resisted the impulse. Instead, she deliberately spent another moment re-reading a summary of the divorce terms.

She was keeping everything she had before the marriage, which amounted to a remote country property she had been bequeathed after the premature deaths of her parents. Reginald had been arm-twisted into giving her a single lump sum payment, a generous amount that wouldn't dent his duchy's coffers but he complained about all the same. Beatrice was also supposed to receive the deed to their London townhouse, but she now noticed that the property was missing from the settlement. She set down the pen. "Reginald." Her tone was sharp. Her soon-to-be former husband, both of their solicitors, and Katherine, the woman who would soon be Reginald's second wife and new duchess, flinched.

Reginald's gray-streaked brows rose too high for him to be truly surprised. "Yes?"

"I am not signing this. We agreed I would keep the townhouse."

Katherine opened her mouth to reply, closing it with a look from Reginald. "We decided it would be best for me to increase my monetary settlement to you and I will keep the townhouse," he said.

Beatrice glanced at the decree again. "The increase is hardly equal to the value of a home in Mayfair," she replied icily.

"My solicitor has informed me that the increase is reasonable in exchange for the property. Besides, you have a family estate to return to."

"Clifford House is in Rainfield! It's the middle of nowhere!" she protested. "It hasn't been used in decades!"

"Local staff has maintained the estate. I made sure of it. I also arranged for it to be cleaned in anticipation of your arrival." Reginald pinned her with his customary smug look, lips slightly upturned in a way that told Beatrice that this entire miserable affair would go exactly as he intended.

She threw the pen across the decree. Drops of black ink splattered across the page, reminding her of blood. "I will not sign it unless I am guaranteed the house. You can buy another." With an accusatory look at Katherine, she snapped, "Both of you will still have more money than God after this. Let me have my house!"

Reginald's voice came out a low growl. The very air seemed to change, the temperature dropping a few degrees. "If you insist on being difficult, I will take everything, including Clifford House, and leave you penniless. I can do that. The law says I can. I am being kind to you, Beatrice."

Her breath caught, her retort sticking in her throat. She knew what he said was true. They were not and never would be, equals. As much as she despised the idea of being banished to Clifford House, it was the only home she had at that moment. Blinking away tears, she snatched the pen and signed her name.

Reginald gave her a predatory smile of satisfaction, his expression reminding her of a small child whose tantrum had been successful.

She supposed he *was* just an overgrown child. She ached to throw the pen in his face. Instead, she hefted its weight in her hand. Real silver, with an onyx inset at one end. She tucked it in her hand. "I'm keeping this."

Reginald shrugged, the motion belied by his wide grin. "As you wish. Our business is concluded, Lady Beatrice."

Beatrice flinched at the mention of her maiden name's old title. Of course, she had known she would be losing her title of duchess upon the divorce, relegated again to being the mere daughter of a dead viscount. But she had also been Beatrice Duff for over half her life, and shedding Reginald's name would take some time to get used to.

"You won't be using the name 'Duff,' will you?" Katherine piped up, speaking for the first time.

Beatrice glared at her. "I would rather die."

A blush touched her cheeks. "Good. Having two Mrs. Duffs or two Duchess of Bewdleys—Duchesses of Bewdley?" Katherine's smooth brow wrinkled a little as she wrestled with the grammar. "Having two would be confusing."

"Also illegal," Reginald said too cheerfully for Beatrice's taste. To his solicitor, he asked, "Is it done?"

Reginald's solicitor was already gathering the pages of the settlement. "My Lord, I will file all this post haste, but yes, it is complete."

"Excellent." Reginald bowed his head at Beatrice, still wearing a smug smile she wanted to slap off his face. "I wish you the best in life, Lady Beatrice. If you have any further inquiries about the settlement, please speak to my solicitor."

Without a backward glance, Reginald, his solicitor, and Katherine swept from the room. Only Beatrice and Mr. Simpson remained. He was an abrupt, short-tempered man, with little patience for a woman client being divorced, even if she was a duchess. She supposed she should be a little grateful to him for saving her family's assets.

She stared at the closed door, a film of tears crowding

her eyes. To her mortification, a couple slid down her cheeks. Rising, she allowed Mr. Simpson to help her into her coat. "Thank you," she said over the lump in her throat.

"It was not my pleasure, exactly, but I tried my best to mitigate the financial damage to you. Contrary to the stereotypes of my profession, I am not happy to contribute to the suffering of others. I truly tried to keep the townhouse in your possession, Your Grace."

"There's no need for honorifics anymore."

"The decree has not yet been filed. You're still the Duchess of Bewdley until then. I did not know until shortly before you did that the Duke would keep the townhouse. His solicitor threatened to tear up the entire settlement and take everything from you if we protested."

Beatrice withdrew an embroidered handkerchief from her reticule, noting the stitches spelled out her married name's initials. Dabbing at her eyes, she said, "I should not be surprised at Reginald's trickery, yet I am. I appreciate your help all the same."

Mr. Simpson looked away for a few seconds.

Beatrice's heart sank further than she would have ever expected. What horrible news was he about to deliver now?

"Your things are being packed as we speak. You are not to return to the house today, or ever. The Duke has arranged a room for you at the Savoy, after which you are to retreat to either Clifford House or a property of your choosing that he does not own."

Any feelings of benevolence she'd earlier harbored evaporated. "You didn't think to inform me of this until now?"

"I was not aware of this development until five minutes before you arrived for the signing!"

Outrage colored her words. "Five minutes was enough time to tell me that I would be cast out of the marital home I was promised!"

Mr. Simpson's voice was cold. "This is not an uncommon situation for divorced wives to find themselves in. You should be grateful you have the funds to keep yourself afloat, Your Grace."

Grateful to her husband for merely divorcing her instead of poisoning her. Grateful to a solicitor—another man—for ensuring she could keep her property acquired before marriage, that if the universe was just, he shouldn't have had a claim to. Grateful to men just for existing. She matched his tone, putting as much frost into it as she could. "Have my things sent to Clifford House."

"I thought you wanted to stay in London for the time being."

Beatrice put as much authority into her voice as she could muster. As Mr. Simpson pointed out, she was still a duchess until the settlement was filed. "I do not wish to stay in this cesspit of a city any longer. Have my things sent to Clifford House, and arrange my transport to it at once. I will require passage aboard a dirigible. There is an airfield close enough to it that I will be able to hire a steam cab to get me the rest of the way there."

Mr. Simpson blinked, clearly surprised at Beatrice's about-face. "Of course. I will take care of everything. You'll be booked on the first flight out of London."

Buttoning her coat, she pasted a smile to her face, hoping her tears hadn't made her face turn red. "Thank you."

Without another word, she left the office.

CHAPTER 2

Night had fallen when Beatrice found herself under the awning of the Herefordshire airfield's comptroller's office. A spring storm began shortly before the dirigible anchored, leaving Beatrice soaked as soon as she walked down its gangplank. Her traveling dress was saturated with rain and the feathers in her bonnet drooped, a nice accessory to her ruined hairstyle, she thought ruefully. At her feet rested a small trunk of her most important possessions. The rest of her things would be brought to Clifford House in the following days. If *she* could be brought to Clifford House in Rainfield first. Her assertion to Mr. Simpson the day before about finding transport to the village from the airfield came back to taunt her. She glanced on either side of her again, willing the vehicle he said he had arranged for her to appear. The dirigible had landed over an hour ago and the steam cab should have been waiting. She pulled her watch from her skirt pocket, squinting to read the numerals in the dim light offered by flickering gas lamps mounted to the wall behind her. It was nearing ten o'clock. Beatrice should be at Clifford House by now, perhaps soothing her bruised soul with a glass of brandy from the bottle in her trunk.

The airfield's comptroller opened the door, startling her. "You certain you don't want to wait inside?" he asked. His voice was loose and grizzled, making her suspect that he had had a tipple or two himself.

The smell inside the office had been abominable, reeking of stale tobacco smoke and livestock. The comptroller himself also raked his eyes over her form when she presented her exit ticket to him, as though he was looking for gaps in her clothing. A shudder rolled through her. "No, thank you."

"I got a leg of mutton to share, if you want some."

Ugh. She pasted a smile to her face and was about to offer another polite rejection when the sound of hoofbeats reached her ears. Uttering a silent prayer to a God she hadn't believed in since she was a girl, she leaned away from the wall, daring to stick her head out from under the awning. Rain pelted her and a voice in the back of her mind chided her that her bonnet would be ruined forever.

A carriage approached the airfield at a rapid clip, drawn by a pair of horses. Stopping in front of the comptroller's office, a figure jumped down from the driver's seat and doffed his hat. His features were shadowy in the gaslamp's light. "I'm looking for the Duchess of Bewdley."

Beatrice was no longer the duchess, nor had she been expecting to be conveyed to Clifford House in an old-fashioned carriage, but she would accept his help, all the same. "I am she." Technically, it was a lie, but she wasn't about to correct him.

He nodded, then plopped his wet hat back on his head. "My apologies for the long wait, Your Grace. My cab for hire is having some troubles in the rain and it took longer than I thought it would for me to get the horses out, and oh, my God, I'm babbling while the rain's drowning you." He closed the short distance between the office and carriage. He grabbed her trunk like it weighed nothing. Over his shoulder, he asked, "Do you have any other luggage?"

"No."

"You're a duchess?" slurred the comptroller.

She didn't answer, instead following the driver to his carriage. Opening the carriage, he hefted it inside, then held the door open for her. "Apologies for not having an umbrella, Your Grace. It has not been a good night for me."

At least he was friendly. "I am not fussed with that, Mister ..."

"Tisdale."

"Mr. Tisdale, I did not think to bring one with me, either." She let him help her into the back of the carriage. "I was in a hurry when I left London and it didn't cross my mind to bring one. Rather silly of me, wasn't it?"

A pair of flameless candles burned in the carriage, highlighting the lines crisscrossing his ruddy face like a map. Light blue eyes kindly regarded her beneath a pair of graying brows. "I'm sorry, all the same. I'm to take you to Clifford House, yes? That's what the cable said."

"Do you know where it is?"

"Of course. My wife and I have kept house there for years. I'll have you there in an hour. Roads are a bit muddy."

"Please take your time, Mr. Tisdale."

"Appreciated, Your Grace." He motioned to close the carriage door. Beatrice reached for it with a gloved hand, blocking it. His brows raised in surprise.

"It's just Mrs. Duff now," she said quietly. Although she wasn't certain that was her name now. Should a divorced woman revert to her maiden name? She and Mr. Simpson hadn't discussed that. At thirty-nine years old, she would feel a bit foolish going by Miss Hall.

Mr. Tisdale, to his everlasting credit, didn't ask further questions about her new status. "Understood. I'll have you at Clifford House shortly, Mrs. Duff."

~

As THE CARRIAGE lumbered over the sodden road, Beatrice had time to ruminate over her upcoming arrival to Clifford House. A knot of dread lodged itself in her stomach at the memories of the place, an ancestral home of her mother's. It hadn't been entailed, so when her brother unexpectedly died and the viscountcy went to one of her second cousins, there had been no one to fight her for the property. No one except Reginald, and she suspected his threats to take it in the divorce were false. He had never so much as set foot on the estate.

Beatrice hadn't been there since she was a girl. Despite Mr. Simpson's assurances that the estate had been maintained in her absence, she was nervous about what she would find there.

Or who she would find there.

She unpinned her sodden hat and leaned back against the carriage wall. A memory of the angel surfaced, the boy she had been told over and over again didn't exist even though she had presented fistfuls of downy white feathers he left in his wake. Her parents and brother thought her mad, with her father sternly telling her to stay out of the chicken coop. Beatrice hadn't even known where the coop was.

She had been nine years old when she saw him in passing in the nearby woods. At first, Beatrice thought she might have imagined him. Then she wandered away from the house the next day, finding him playing in a cave on a nearby beach. He was a child, although she couldn't guess his exact age, and spoke passable English. They'd whiled away an afternoon, sharing a newspaper-wrapped sandwich the Clifford House cook prepared for Beatrice that she'd stashed in her dress pocket. He hadn't looked like the illustrations of the angels she'd seen in the family children's Bible, but the pictures of the animals aboard Noah's Ark hadn't resembled anything she'd ever seen, so she overlooked that. He had beautiful wings that poked through cutouts in his long blue robe that reminded her of a nightshirt. They weren't the delicate gossamer wings she associated with fairies in her favorite books, but broad things that extended past his bony shoulders, the fine white feathers fluffy. What she could see of his arms and legs were covered in fine, light-colored fur. Beatrice could only vaguely recall his face, only remembering big dark eyes that were nearly black, and a crooked beak of a nose. When she told her parents later in the day that she saw him again, she was forbidden to leave the house and when they returned to London, a doctor was summoned.

A shudder rippled through her at the memory of her visits with the doctor.

I should have never mentioned the angel to anyone. He'd been harmless and Beatrice was a lonely child, the oft-forgotten second child and a girl to boot, too useless to be a spare to her older brother. She'd been thrilled to have a playmate for once. When she had been convinced by Dr. Shepard that he was nothing but a figment of her imagination, she had been devastated. Now she was returning to the place where she had been accused of being mad. She squeezed her eyes shut, as if doing so she could erase her memories of the angel, the doctor, Clifford House itself.

Beatrice must have dozed off, because her eyes flew open when the carriage came to a hard stop, making her lurch forward. Fumbling with her hat, she quickly pinned it back in place, noting that the feathers were drying. She didn't hear rain drumming off the roof, a positive sign. When Mr. Tisdale opened the door, the pleasant scent of petrichor hung in the air, the smell of spring.

Perhaps this exile to the countryside wouldn't be so terrible.

Mr. Tisdale helped her out of the carriage, leaving her on the drive while he reached for her trunk. Beatrice stared at the brick house before her, smaller than she remembered but still imposing. Stretching three floors, it was flanked on either side by turrets, their dormer windows dark. The generous front garden was tidy, albeit bare aside from patchy grass and neatly trimmed shrubbery. It reminded her of an unloved relative, forgotten by their family, maintained by the family's solicitor out of a sense of duty rather than love.

"A meal has been set out for you, waiting in the icebox. My wife has left a few things for you to nibble on until she can stop by in the next day or so. Nothing fancy, though," Mr. Tisdale announced as he hauled the trunk.

"I'm sure it will be delicious." She followed him up the drive, up the single stair that led to the front double doors. The door's green paint had peeled in spots, visible under the lamp mounted beside it. With a start, Beatrice realized she didn't have a key to the house.

Mr. Tisdale withdrew one from his coat pocket. He opened the door and shoved the trunk inside, then stood out of the way to let her pass. He handed the key to her.

"Thank you."

He switched on a wall-mounted gas lamp, filling the foyer with yellow light. "Was my pleasure, Your Grace."

"Mrs. Duff," she corrected him. "I am no longer a duchess."

"Still the daughter of an earl, are you not, my lady?"

"A viscount."

"Viscount, that's right. Shall I take this upstairs? The largest suite has been prepared for you."

Beatrice tugged at her gloves, the damp leather sticking to her skin. "I would appreciate that, Mr. Tisdale."

He wiped his brow with the back of his hand. "After that, I'll be moving on home, if that's all right with you. Old stone cottage with apple trees in the front. You can't miss it. About two miles from here, if you need us."

She smiled. "Thank you. I'm certain I can manage on my own for a few days."

Mr. Tisdale carried the trunk up the main staircase without asking for her approval, taking a liberty that would have had her parents or Reginald in an apoplectic fit about servants' manners and using stairs meant for them. Beatrice didn't have it in her to care. She shucked off her own coat, then noticed there wasn't anywhere to hang it. With a sigh, she followed Mr. Tisdale.

CHAPTER 3

THE CHILL COMING in from the beach was intolerable. Leo huddled in the low-ceilinged cave. He'd wrapped woolen blanket around himself in a futile attempt to keep warm. Ann and Harold Tisdale had promised to look into another living situation now that he had been all but evicted from Clifford House's grounds. He still knew something that would both meet his needs and keep him from drawing attention to himself would be difficult to find, if not impossible.

How had his ancestors tolerated the cold? None of them would have had access to a warm keep or cottage, let alone the grand country house he did, a magnificent structure that had been all but abandoned. They must have found a way to survive and thrive. Tugging the blanket around him tighter, he prayed again for the early April chill to leave once and for all, or at least for the season.

I miss my nest.

Technically, the pieces he'd used to cobble it together belonged to the duchess who had finally decided to grace

Clifford House and Herefordshire with her presence. He still considered the shredded mattress and bedding to be his. Even if the mattress was stuffed with feathers, which he supposed should probably be disturbing to a being like him, yet wasn't. That was probably the Tisdales' influence, along with his wearing clothing. With a sigh, he looked down at his trousers. They were all but ruined after being exposed to the elements. He didn't even want to think about his poor linen shirt and the dirt stains that would never come out. The Tisdales had also left some novels with him as a way to pass the time until he could find somewhere else to live. They were wrapped in clean oilcloth for protection, a neat stack he kept next to him. They were a poor distraction for someone who preferred to create music. He missed Clifford House's piano.

If my parents could see me now, how soft I've become, they would molt on the spot.

A fly landed on his exposed neck, the first of the season that he could recall. He reached for it, the primal part of him eager to eat it, but the wily bastard flew off before he could grab it. A couple of feathers fell out instead. Forget his late parents, he was molting from the stress.

He leaned back against the cave wall, and prayed the Tisdales would return soon with news that the duchess was gone.

BEATRICE HAD BEEN TOO exhausted to examine the house when Mr. Tisdale took his leave. She woke up to sunshine peeking through the curtains in the bedroom that had been prepared for her, an unexpected sight amid such dreary spring weather. "Hopefully, this is a good sign," she murmured as she climbed out of the tester that had once belonged to her parents. It was a trifle smaller than she remembered it, the old-fashioned bed coverings faded.

Her trunk was unpacked, save for the nightgown she wore to bed. Digging through it, she pulled out a plain blouse and a pair of sensible trousers, the kind made for lady aviators. God above, but Reginald had hated seeing women wearing trousers. She bit back a smile as she dressed, the knowledge that at least she could now wear what she wanted without hearing her husband complain about it oddly comforting. She tied her hair back at the nape of her neck with a ribbon, letting her long blonde tresses loose down her back. With a critical eye in the looking glass, she noticed that her temples and part were more silvery than they were six months ago, which she blamed on Reginald.

The Tisdales had left a couple of days' worth of meals in the icebox, and as she prepared breakfast, she was suddenly grateful that she wasn't completely useless. Beatrice could survive on her own without a lady's maid or cook. She could boil an egg, prepare her own toast and tea. She made a second cup after she cleaned up her breakfast mess, and with it in hand, set out to inspect the rest of the house.

It wasn't just the tester that was smaller than she remembered. It was the entire house. The remaining furniture was covered in dusty white cloths, and she vaguely remembered her parents talking about selling some of it to repay debts. Which debts, she had no idea, as she had been largely shielded from the financial doings of her family. To her surprise, she found the music room clean, its grand piano shined to a high gloss, the keys spotless. When she touched one, the sound that came out seemed to be in tune. The matching bench had a flowery embroidered cushion spread on it, a deep indentation in the middle a sign of it being well-used. A couple of small feathers rested on top, sending a chill down Beatrice's spine.

They look just like the ones from the angel.

With shaking fingers, she plucked them from the cushion and inspected them. Ordinary white feathers, downy in her hands, exactly the kind used for cushions. She forced herself to breathe, to quell her heart that now thundered against her ribs. The room and piano's upkeep must have been the work of the Tisdales. She couldn't bring herself to be upset at them if they were using it. The piano was a fine instrument and deserved to be played. Glancing at the feathers again, she stuck them in her trouser pocket. A few pieces of sheet music rested on the piano's shelf, mostly Mendelssohn, but she spied a copy of "Daisy Bell," when she picked them up and leafed through them. They were well-used, the edges of the broadsides yellowing and soft, like they had been played over and over again. Beatrice returned them to the shelf, and would have turned away had something over the exposed strings not caught her attention. She peered inside, the blinked in astonishment at the sight.

Another feather, this one deep gray and the length of her hand.

Her breath caught. Afraid her legs might give way beneath her, she slumped on the bench, the cushion catching her before she could slide to the floor. *It's just a feather. A giant feather. It means nothing.* "I'm being ridiculous," Beatrice said aloud, hoping the sound of her own voice would quell the uneasiness that swept through her. She closed her eyes for a moment, reminding herself that she was awake, that she wasn't dreaming. When she rose again and looked into the piano, she saw the feather was still there. Taking care not to disturb the strings, she plucked it out. It was just as soft as the white ones in her pocket.

Reginald must have planned this.

He had known about her delusion about the angel boy —he had been friends with her late older brother, who had told him about Beatrice's medical treatment for it when they were children. She and Reginald had never discussed it beyond a humiliating family supper when she was four-teen or so, but he had been aware. He must have had the feathers planted here as a final way to tell her to fuck right off. A reminder of her place as a madwoman no one else wanted.

A clanging of chimes wrenched a shriek from her, and she nearly dropped the feather. She'd all but forgotten the doorbell, one of the house's few modern amenities. Rushing from the music room, she placed a hand over her heart in a feeble attempt to bring its beat back to normal.

She found a woman on the front doorstep who looked to be in her seventies, gray wisps of hair peeking out from beneath her bonnet. Her sensible brown wool skirt had a few speckles of mud at the hem. Face splitting into a grin, she said, "You must be the Duchess of Bewdley. I'm Ann Tisdale. I believe my husband drove you home last night?"

To Beatrice's relief, her voice came out steady, giving no indication that she'd nearly been startled to death. "It's only Mrs. Duff now."

Mrs. Tisdale's smile didn't falter. "I heard about your misfortune, and I offer my condolences to you. May I come in? You haven't been here for quite a while and I thought you might want an expert guide to this old house. The kitchen appliances are going to be much older than what you have in London."

Beatrice didn't have the energy for company, but she still pasted a smile on her face. It wouldn't do to be impolite to someone who was willing to help her. She'd had so few allies since Reginald announced his intention to divorce her. She stepped aside. "Please, do come in."

CHAPTER 4

Their footsteps were muffled by the blue runner underfoot as they walked to the kitchen. "You'll have to forgive me, but I don't remember any of the staff from when I was a girl," Beatrice apologized. "I can't begin to tell you how much I appreciate you and Mr. Tisdale's maintenance of the house."

"Your father and later the Duke have always compensated us fairly," Mrs. Tisdale replied. It was indelicate to discuss finances, but today, Beatrice didn't mind. They walked into the kitchen. "Truly, it's not a bother. Just some occasional dusting. There aren't any chickens or flowerbeds anymore, of course, so there's much less to look after."

The mention of chickens reminded Beatrice of the feathers in her pocket. As Mrs. Tisdale unloaded her basket in the icebox, she wondered how to bring them up. *They're probably from the cushions, you dolt.* But that long gray feather … she withdrew it, running her fingers over its soft edge. Cushions weren't stuffed with anything so large. She didn't even know of a bird species that would produce them in that size. "Are there any other birds on the property?" she asked. "I have to admit I'm not terribly familiar with ornithology."

Mrs. Tisdale's back stiffened for a fraction of a second. If Beatrice hadn't been watching so closely, she would have missed it. Turning around, the older woman had a smile on her face that looked a little forced. It fell when she saw the feather in Beatrice's hand. Quickly recovering, she replied, "No, none that I'm aware of. Where did you find that?"

"Stuck in the piano strings."

"Oh! Silly me, I must have knocked it aside when I was dusting. I hope you don't mind the impertinence. Mr. Tisdale and I have enjoyed playing it. We're not especially talented, mind you, but the music does help pass the time. The little old spinet in our house is no match for the piano you have here. Do you play, Your Grace?"

Mrs. Tisdale's smile had returned, although her gaze didn't meet Beatrice's. *She's hiding something.* Sidestepping the housekeeper's use of her old title, Beatrice replied, "No. I have a tin ear, unfortunately."

"The viscount played, did he not?"

She wasn't sure which viscount Mrs. Tisdale was referring to. Her father and brother both played well enough. "Yes." Stroking the pad of her thumb against the feather's edge again, she marveled at its size and Mrs. Tisdale's obvious shock at seeing it.

An insane notion struck her, one that hinted she might not have been delusional so many years ago. What if she had been correct about the angel? She'd known deep in her bones that she had played with him, shared her sandwich with him. She *knew*, despite the treatments her parents had foisted on her. If Mrs. Tisdale knew something about the angel, Beatrice didn't want to let on that she suspected something. She returned the feather to her pocket and steered the conversation away from birds. "My father tried to teach me to play. I think he would have liked it if I'd been proficient in anything musical or artistic, but that eluded me, too."

The housekeeper visibly relaxed. "We're hardly skilled, although my Harold does enjoy his carols at Christmas. Can I get you a cup of tea?"

"I can manage."

Mrs. Tisdale's hazel eyes widened. "But, Your Grace . . ."

Beatrice shook her head. "I am no longer a duchess. Didn't Mr. Tisdale tell you the Duke divorced me? Threw me over for a twenty-year-old chit who can give him the heir he thinks he deserves?" The words flew out of her before she could think better of them. She clapped her hand over her mouth, shocked into silence. Neither woman spoke for a moment. The silence between them was palpable, confirmation that Beatrice had just committed an unforgivable sin in the aristocracy. Two, as a matter of fact: being divorced and talking about being divorced.

Mrs. Tisdale spoke first. "What an utter *bastard* your husband is."

Beatrice hadn't expected to hear such vehemence from her. If Reginald was here now, she thought the housekeeper might tear him limb from limb in front of her, then offer to help Beatrice hide the body.

Beatrice couldn't tell if she was on the verge of laughter or tears or both. "Yes, he is." She took a deep breath, collecting herself. "Let me get some tea for us. Do you take sugar?"

~

It was early afternoon when Mrs. Tisdale left, with a promise to return in a day or two. Beatrice had found she enjoyed her company. She was kind and plain-spoken, heartily cursing out Reginald to Beatrice's surprise and delight. It felt good to have an ally for once, someone who wouldn't blame her for Reginald's wandering eye.

Still, Beatrice wasn't sorry to see the housekeeper leave, not when she still had some investigating to do. The sky was gray, fog hanging in the air when she let herself out of the servants' door in the kitchen to the sprawling estate grounds. It was the kind of afternoon that could see either a massive downpour or the clouds splitting apart to reveal the sun at a moment's notice. Beatrice found an old mackintosh with a hood shoved in a closet and slipped it on, just in case. Her boots were still damp from the rain the night before, but they would have to do.

She'd met the angel in a copse of trees about a quarter mile from the house, she recalled. It didn't take long to remember the route she'd taken so many years ago, the paths growing over with vegetation tipped with green buds. The copse was so thick with bare brambles that she found it nearly impossible to walk through as the thorns pulled at her mackintosh, and besides that, it was smaller than she recalled. She could see through it to the other side, where an untended stretch of field waited. There was nowhere for an angel to hide here. "Except up," she murmured to herself, then gazed into the trees. Still largely bare of leaves, they were empty save for a bird that rested on a branch far above her head.

She cut around the trees to the field, a sense of dejection washing over her. A part of her had truly expected the angel boy to still be here, or at least leave evidence of his existence other than the feathers in the music room and

Mrs. Tisdale's reaction to the one in her hand, she remembered.

Beyond the field was a beach that abetted a lake she had never been allowed to go near. Her parents had been deathly afraid of deep water, a fear that had been passed on to Beatrice, but she kept walking toward it, determined to see what she had been forbidden to approach all those years ago. A fog hung over the water, perhaps a sign of impending rain. On impulse, she pulled the mackintosh's hood over her hair. It was a dreary-looking spot, she decided as her boots crunched over pebbles. Beatrice had only been to one beach in her life, one in Calais, where she and Reginald honeymooned. It had had a warm sand bar, dotted with people hiding from the blazing sun under gigantic umbrellas, huge clockwork fans whirring to keep visitors cool.

A small cliff crested the far side of the beach, a couple of cave mouths visible from where she stood. A smile crept across her face at the thought of pirates hiding treasure in them. Perhaps that was the real reason her parents forbade her from playing there. Surely, there had to be a way for a pirate ship to wind its way from the sea to a lake in the middle of nowhere. Beatrice cautiously approached the first opening, noting with disappointment that it was too shallow for anything or anyone to use. The second was about twenty feet away, larger than the first, the size of a doorway. She paused, smelling the air.

Fire.

Someone had lit a fire near here recently. A curious excitement welled in her. Taking care to hide the sound of her footfalls, she made her way toward the cave mouth and stuck her head inside.

"Ann? Is that you? This is absolutely intolerable…"

The voice that came from the cave was masculine, with a distinctive Herefordshire clip.

Beatrice's heart stilled for a moment until her eyes adjusted to the sight inside.

A feathered head, a face that was strangely human in the dim light offered by a flameless candle held in a fluffy hand. There were a pair of black eyes, wide with shock as he realized that whoever stood in the cave mouth wasn't this Ann woman.

Beatrice took a step back, nearly stumbling in her shock. She had been right, all those years ago. "The angel boy," she said softly, blinking a couple of times to be certain her eyes weren't playing a trick on her.

His face twisted in obvious terror. He rose, dropping the candle. "Who are you?"

CHAPTER 5

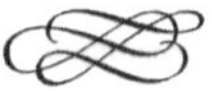

WHEN LEO WAS SMALL, he'd held a fascination for books of all kinds, an eagerness to learn about the human world that he was mostly forbidden from exploring. He'd loved reading about birds and the parallels between them and himself. Worryingly, they could die of fright or shock, and as he stared at the stranger in the cave entrance, he thought he might have that in common with the poor creatures. His heart stilled. For a moment, he expected to crash face first to the cave's floor.

"The angel boy," the woman who definitely wasn't Ann Tisdale said, her voice breathless.

Leo had also thought that he would definitely be full of bravado and witty comebacks should he ever encounter a stranger, a notion that failed him now. If he confirmed that he was an angel, she might leave him alone. But then she might return with other people who believed in angels and that would bring a whole new kind of headache to him, the Tisdales, and the few other people in Rainfield who knew of his existence. Drat it all, he should have found somewhere else to hide. She wasn't holding a weapon that he could see. She didn't seem afraid of him, which he wasn't sure was a good sign or not. "No," he replied. "I'm not an angel."

"But you're real," she said.

He could see her features clearly, his superior eyesight being something he had in common with birds. Her expression wasn't one of fear or disgust, but curiosity. Her lips upturned in an expression that wasn't quite a smile, but vindication, perhaps? Like she had been proven correct about something?

She took a cautious step into the cave.

Leo shrank back involuntarily, clutching his blanket to him like a shield.

"We met before," she said, voice soft. "About thirty years or so ago? Please tell me you remember playing with me in the woods."

Leo's breath caught. A memory surfaced of him as a boy, newly turned over to the Tisdales' custody and meeting a little girl close to his age near Clifford House. They'd whiled away an afternoon playing together. Ann had been furious when she found out about their encounter.

"I gave you half my sandwich," the woman added.

His response was automatic. "Tomato." He didn't know why he remembered that detail, yet he did.

"Yes. My name is Beatrice. I don't think we ever introduced ourselves, or if we did, I've forgotten." She took another step closer to him, bringing with her a faint scent of soap that smelled finer than anything the Tisdales left for him in Clifford House.

"Why are you here?" The question slipped from him before he could think it over.

She blinked in surprise. "I own Clifford House. I've come home, in a manner of speaking." The last sentence was spoken with a note of bitterness, as if she truly didn't want to return to Herefordshire.

Panic struck Leo with the force of a kick to the gut. She was returning to claim the only home he had? It took every ounce of self-control he had not to wail in anguish. "I see."

"What's your name?" she pressed.

She already knew of his existence. There was no point in lying about his name. "Leo."

"Leo what?"

"Beatrice what?" he countered.

A ghost of a smile appeared on her full lips. "Formerly Beatrice Duff, Duchess of Bewdley. Now, I'm just Beatrice Hall again. Now, Leo what?"

"Leo Tisdale, I suppose. Isn't it customary to call you Lady Beatrice?"

To his surprise, she shrugged. "My father and brother are dead and the title went to a cousin I've met perhaps half a dozen times in my life. I've been exiled to the countryside by my former husband. There's nothing ladylike about me now."

Despite the inelegance of her silvery blond hair held off her face in a simple braid and her trousers, there was a regal air to her, that of a woman used to getting her way. Her posture was impossibly correct under her oversized camel-colored mackintosh. Bright spots of color bloomed on her cheeks, full lips pink, a smattering of freckles across her nose. Big gray eyes fringed with light lashes peered at him beneath a pair of finely knit blond brows. He recognized her as the little girl he'd once played with.

She withdrew a long gray feather from her mackintosh pocket. "Is this yours?"

He recognized it immediately. Mortification washed over him in a wave. "Yes," he mumbled.

"Do you want it back?"

He stared at her for a moment, agape. "No, thank you."

"I found it in the music room. It was stuck in the piano strings. That's what made me think I might not have gone mad all those years ago."

Of everything she could have said to him, he wasn't expecting that. "I beg your pardon?"

She looked away, but not before he saw a flash of sadness in her eyes. "Never mind. I knew I hadn't imagined you, is all. Do you play the piano? Is that why I found feathers in that room?"

"Yes. It's a hobby I enjoy."

"Have you been living in Clifford House in my absence?"

She didn't sound angry, but Leo didn't know her well enough to be certain. "Yes. I—I had nowhere else to go. The Tisdales said you never visited but sent enough money to maintain it."

"I see. Why are you here now?"

"Why are *you* here now?" he returned.

"Exile, as I already told you."

"I suppose the same could be said of my circumstances."

She put her hands on her hips. When she spoke, her voice was indignant. "Are you telling me the Tisdales have left you in a cave by yourself while I'm in residence?"

"You're making it sound worse than it is. Their house is too small and too close to the village for me to stay there and none of their friends who know about me had the space. They're working to find somewhere else for me." Besides that, he should be able to thrive in a space such as this, with a proper nest of his own made from twigs and grasses instead of a destroyed mattress. Spending his life with humans had ruined his natural instincts.

She pinched the bridge of her nose between her fingers. "I can't believe this," she muttered.

"You were rather vindicated by my existence not ten minutes ago."

"No, not that. Look, Leo, you aren't suited for this." She gestured around the cave.

"Yes, I am." The protest was weak. He looked down at his dirt-stained clothing and sighed.

"You're an angel who plays piano and wears clothes. Those things are incompatible with living in a cave."

"Only two of those attributes apply to me."

Beatrice raised an eyebrow in a silent question.

"I'm not an angel," he explained.

She looked like she was trying to decide if it was polite to ask him what he was. "Understood," she finally replied.

"I'm a gryphon."

"Gryphons are real?"

Now it was his turn to feel flummoxed. "Not a minute ago, you thought angels were real!"

"Are they?"

"I don't know. I've never met one."

She nodded, full lips thinning as she considered this new development. "Even if you don't have celestial origins, I … you can't stay here. Where did you stay in Clifford House?"

His heart suddenly increased tempo, slamming against his ribs. An odd sense of hope crested in him. "There's a small room on the west side of the house that I was fond of. Blue and gray draperies and rugs?"

"Yes, that was a room once used by my Uncle Louis. Did you sleep in that bed?"

"No, I have a nest."

"Good. Uncle Louis died in it and my father saw replacing the mattress as an unnecessary expense." A shudder rippled through her. "You can return to Clifford House, if you want."

He did, desperately. He nearly blurted out his thanks, stopping himself in time. "Why do you want me at the house?"

"Because no matter what my former husband might say to society, I'm not a heartless monster. You have also just vindicated me after decades of being told I was mad. The least I can do is offer you refuge again. God knows I have the space."

"I'm a monster," he pointed out.

She gave another half-shrug. "Have you ever sent one of your children to an asylum for treatment?"

"I don't have any children."

"But if you did, would you do that?" she pressed.

He didn't know, but he had the impression that if he said yes, she would leave him in the cave. She'd mentioned being treated for madness after they played together. "No."

"Have you divorced your wife for the sin of merely getting older?"

"I've never had a wife."

"But if you did ..."

"No! Is that what you mean by 'former husband'? He isn't dead, just divorced?"

"Just ..." She closed her eyes. He must have misstepped again. "Yes, we have been divorced. I would have been better off if I'd poisoned him."

The vehemence in her voice struck a chord of nervousness in him. "Are you in the habit of poisoning others?"

"No. It didn't occur to me that I should have done that until he told me he was keeping our London townhouse, which he originally promised I could keep."

"If I may be honest, I don't think I want to live with a poisoner," Leo replied.

"I don't have the nerve for it, anyway. So, Leo, do you want to come home?"

He hated this makeshift nest, hated the cave, hated the damp chill coming off the lake. He was losing feathers from the stress and he worried about his piano skills atrophying further. "Yes."

"Then gather your things and come with me." She eyed the firepit. "Is this out? I don't want to set the countryside alight."

"It's out. I'm not very good at keeping a fire going."

"That's a pity, because the house is damp and until now, I had servants to light them for me. Clifford House is missing too many modern conveniences for my taste." She massaged her temples. "My apologies. I don't mean to complain."

Leo rose, noting at his full height he was easily a foot taller than Beatrice, who wasn't particularly short herself. He hoped she couldn't see his stained clothes in the cave darkness. "I don't have much. I was waiting for Ann to return with some more supplies."

"Should we leave her a note?"

He had a few novels he could tear pages out of, but nothing to write with. "I don't have a pencil."

"No matter. We'll tell her ourselves the next time she or Mr. Tisdale visits." He gathered his meager possessions in an old leather satchel Ann found in a closet. "I believe that's Uncle Louis's favorite satchel."

"Did he die in bed with it?" Leo folded his blanket and neatly packed it away. When he looked at Beatrice, she had a curious expression on her face. His claws, he realized. He had clawed hands, the backs and fingers dappled with fine tan-colored fur.

"He did not, to the best of my knowledge."

Satchel in hand, Leo stretched his wings to work out a

cramp before slipping on his overcoat. He held his breath as he did so. The garment stank of smoke and lake water, offensive to his constitution. Beatrice's eyes widened at the sight before his wings were tucked away. "My hat is somewhere at the bottom of the lake," he said apologetically. "The wind got it last night."

"I'll see that you get a replacement. Let's go." A peal of thunder sounded in the distance. "I don't want to get caught in the rain again."

CHAPTER 6

As they walked back to the house, a new feeling came over Beatrice. It was a curious mix of elation and satisfaction. As she'd told Leo in the cave, she was finally feeling vindicated that after all these years, she was proven correct about the angel boy. After everything she had been put through by her parents for her belief, after being branded mad and foisted on Reginald, she was walking alongside the object of the scorn heaped on her, the rain lightly misting his feathers. *Not an angel*, she corrected herself. *A gryphon*. Although if she had reported back to her parents that she'd played with a gryphon, their reaction would have been much the same. The house came into view before she spoke. "Can I ask how you came to Herefordshire?"

"My family lived in these parts for many years," Leo replied. "They passed away when I was small. They were friendly with a few human families in the area, people who had kept our existence secret for generations. After my father died, the Tisdales offered to care for me."

"There's no one left of your kind?"

"Not in England, that I know of. There was a ... a kind of plague when I was a child. Something that affected the others breathing, I'm uncertain of the name. My flock slowly died out over a period of years." Leo's reply was clipped, devoid of emotion. He clearly didn't want to discuss his family.

"I'm sorry."

He shrugged and looked away. "I've not had a bad life."

"Until I came here and forced your eviction." She tried to keep her voice light and failed.

"It's your house."

"It was *your* home. I don't need that much space. I don't even know if I'm going to stay in Herefordshire." They had reached the servants' entrance at the back of the kitchen. Leo opened the door before she could, holding it for her. "After you," she said, stalling.

"I'm not so clueless about the society you come from that I can't hold a door open for a lady."

For some reason, that statement sent a flutter through her, as if they were in a ballroom and she'd been waiting for him to ask her to dance. Walking over the threshold, she said, "Thank you." She shucked the mackintosh, returning to it to the peg where she found it, then unbuttoned her damp boots, kicking them off in a most unladylike fashion.

Leo still had his bag in hand, his clothes rumpled and dirty. "Do you wish to have a bath?" she asked. "The house has indoor plumbing."

"I know."

Of course, he would know. She immediately felt foolish. "You do — you do use a bathtub?"

"As opposed to a birdbath?"

"Is that an awkward question to ask?"

"Possibly, but I don't have a large social circle, so I can't say for sure." He smiled, the first time he'd done so since she found him in the cave.

Beatrice could now see his features clearly. He towered over by at least a foot, his body broad. Gray and white wings sprouted from his shoulders through cutouts in his clothing. Light fur covered the backs of his paws and what she could see of his wrists. Fine, downy feathers covered his scalp and small ears that lay close to his head. His face's features, combined with his wings, gave him a human-like quality that made it easy for Beatrice to think she'd met an angel so many years ago. His eyes were large and black beneath a pair of thin, feathery brows, reminding her of the eyes of a canary her mother once had as a pet, without visible pupils. A sharp beak of a nose, the color of freshly churned butter, protruded from his face. His lips were blue-black, fuller than she would have expected from a bird man if she'd thought more about bird features. Realizing she was staring, she gave her head a little shake. "I've had no shortage of people tell me I'm awkward, so I don't know, either. You said you have a preferred room in the west wing?"

"Yes."

"And I will have a word with Mrs. Tisdale the next time she stops by. I can't believe you were left in a cave on the beach!"

"To be fair, my people did spend most of their time outdoors. I'm an anomaly."

On stocking feet, Beatrice headed into the kitchen. "That doesn't reassure me. The Tisdales brought you under their care, raised you like a human child, and then turned you out when you became inconvenient. I wish they had told me."

"What would you have done?"

She had intended to prepare a pot of tea for them to share after he'd taken his bath, but there was a sharp note in his tone and she paused, hand hovering over the brass kettle. "I would have given you my blessing to stay in the house."

Leo didn't look convinced, at least as far as Beatrice could read his expression.

"Do you drink tea?" she asked, needing to change the subject.

He nodded.

"I'll have some ready after you've had your bath."

He looked like he had a rejoinder, but thought better of it. His reply was soft. "Thank you."

Leo half-expected Beatrice or someone to barge into the room while he was bathing, perhaps a constable or a tabloid journalist, but he was left alone. He tried to relax under the water but noted with dismay that he'd lost yet more feathers. It wasn't only the changing season that was the cause of the loss. He had been the most stressed since his mother died when he'd been ordered to leave Clifford House. Having its mistress accept him back into the home did little to assuage his anxiety.

He relaxed a little after he found the rest of his clothing was exactly where he'd left it in a highboy, the extra-long trousers and shirts Ann had so carefully made for him. It felt good to be in clean clothes again, a feeling that didn't leave him when he left his room, smelling like soap instead of wood smoke and the lake. Still, he paused in the corridor and listened for Beatrice. Faintly, he heard her puttering around the kitchen. Did duchesses cook? Everything Ann and Harold had told him said the aristocracy was effectively useless at everyday tasks.

She said she isn't a duchess anymore.

Her husband was no longer in the picture. Her nose, cute little button thing it was, had wrinkled in distaste when she briefly talked about him. Beatrice was a trifle odd, but now that she had left him to his devices, he thought she might be genuinely kind and seemed to have a similar sense of humor as his. Also rather pretty, he decided. Why on earth would a duke not want to be married to her anymore? Perhaps it had been one of those loveless matches made to benefit families rather than the bride and groom. Leo had read about those kinds of arrangements. They were once common in gryphon society, too. He found himself itching to ask her about her marriage but had no idea of the etiquette.

He made his way to the music room, his favorite place in Clifford House and the one he'd missed the most while in the cave. The piano was exactly as he'd left it, the night he'd given an impromptu musicale to Ann and Harold, the sheet music still on the stand. The broadsheets had been rearranged, with "I Dreamt I Dwelt in Marble Halls" resting on top of "Für Elise" and the pages of "The Well-Tempered Clavier" out of order. With a small sigh, he set the sheet music to rights, then sat at the bench. His clawed hands moved smoothly over the ivory keys in scales as Ann had taught him so long ago. He didn't look at the doorway when he heard Beatrice's footsteps in the corridor, then on the floor's polished surface. The pleasant scent of tea reached his beak. Involuntarily, his mouth began to water. He hadn't had a cup in days.

"Will you be put out if I leave this on the piano?" Beatrice asked.

Leo looked at her aghast. She held a tarnished silver

tray in her hands, the kind of serving ware Ann perfunctorily polished once per year. A porcelain pot and a pair of cups rested on it. "Where?" he asked without stopping his scales.

"On the lid?" Her lips twitched, and he realized she was making a joke, albeit a poor attempt at one.

"No. It's open, anyway."

She set the tray on a small wooden table nearby, flanked by chairs on either side.

Ann had arranged the furniture that way for when she and Harold sat in on Leo's performances.

Beatrice sat heavily in one of the chairs, as if she was tired and needed a rest. Perhaps she did. "So, you're a gryphon who plays piano."

He shrugged. He stretched his fingers before starting the G major arpeggio. The notes sang out from the piano, and he noted F-sharp sounded a little off. The hammer's mallet probably needed to be replaced. "I also enjoy reading. Do you play?"

"Not at all. I have no musical talent whatsoever, to the shame of my father. He and my brother could play quite well."

"The viscounts," Leo replied.

"Yes, although they're both gone now. The viscountcy went to a cousin. I only kept this property because it originally belonged to my mother's family and it isn't entailed. Clifford House is the only place I can call home at the moment." She took a delicate sip of tea. Her fine blond brows lifted in surprise. "This isn't terrible."

"You were expecting otherwise?" He launched into the E-major arpeggio.

"I suppose it makes me a snob, but I don't expect things to be the same quality I'm used to in London. Can you play something for me?"

The abrupt change in subject nearly had Leo taking his hands off the keyboard. If he'd been capable of it, he would have blushed. She looked so expectant, almost eager. "Are you serious?"

"I've come all this way in part to find out if you were real after a lifetime of being told you aren't. This is my house and I've paid for the piano's upkeep. You can clearly play, so I would like to hear something."

Leo had played for Ann and Harold hundreds of times, as well as the handful of Rainfield villagers who knew of his existence. Yet this was the first time he felt nervous doing so. Clearing his throat, he asked, "What kind of music do you like?"

"Play your favorite piece for me."

Leo's hands stilled over the keyboard as he considered his options. After a moment, he picked out a few chords, then began "Nocturne in E-Flat Major." He'd always liked Chopin far more than the popular songs Ann and Harold were fond of. Closing his eyes, he forced all thoughts from his mind of how his life had just irrevocably changed, with this woman who was so much more powerful than he ever would be sailing into it and upending it further. His fingers stretched over the keys and he quietly hummed along, keeping the tempo as the notes reached a crescendo, then dove into the final bars of the piece, drifting away in the air like dust motes. He didn't move his hands from the keyboard until the strings stopped vibrating. The room was silent. His hands trembled, claws rattling against the ivories. Emotion formed a lump in his throat that took a few seconds to clear. Everything had changed. He couldn't tell if that was good or bad, didn't know if he should trust Beatrice, as much as a part of him wanted to. He remembered the little girl she'd been. Their whiling away the hours together, playing in the dirt, was one of the few truly happy memories he'd had as a child.

"Leo?" Beatrice's voice was soft. He heard her pad across the floor to the piano, sitting on the bench beside him.

He automatically adjusted his wings to give her more space. It was a tight fit, but he found he didn't mind. Heat radiated off her, a reminder that she was fully human. A warm-blooded mammal. She smelled good, too. Leo had never thought about what *expensive* might smell like until today, and he knew it was whatever duchesses used in their toilette.

"What's wrong?" she asked, voice still quiet.

He shook his head, taking a moment before opening his eyes. "Nothing," he replied thickly.

"I liked your performance. It was beautiful."

"Thank you."

"Are you worried about what I'll do? Because I'm not going to do anything that would harm you, I hope you know that. You can stay here as long as you want."

He desperately wanted to believe her. "What about you?"

She gave him a mirthless smile in response. "What about me? I can't exactly go back to London immediately nor am I certain I want to right now, anyway. I'm going to be scandalized for a long time."

"Surely your husband can't prevent you from returning to your home."

"He can and he has."

"How could the duke do that?"

"Easily. He found another woman he preferred. Anyway, I'd rather not talk about that. There's tea waiting. You said before you wanted some." She rose and returned to her chair. "Come sit with me." There was a defiant set to her jaw, a sparkle in her eyes that wasn't entirely benevolent. Beatrice was a woman scorned, rightfully angry and hurt. Her life was upended against her will just like his.

Leo nodded and stood. He took the seat on the opposite side of the table. Before he could pour a cup for himself, she was already doing it. "We shall have to get along," he said.

Beatrice held out her cup to him. He stared at it blankly. "Have you never toasted anyone before?" she asked.

"No."

"Then we'll do that now. Set your cup's edge against mine."

He did so, the dull clink of the old china edges setting his teeth on edge.

"We will be friends again," she promised.

CHAPTER 7

Leo was skittish. Whether it was because he wasn't used to sharing his space with someone else, that she was a new face to him altogether, or that they were different species, Beatrice couldn't tell. She tried to coordinate her mealtimes with his, encouraging him to join her for dinner or supper, but he demurred. He had eaten a little of what Mrs. Tisdale left for her, and she wondered if he was letting himself go hungry on her account.

Three days after she brought him back to Clifford House, she'd decided to march to the Tisdales house down the road and demand an explanation for Leo having been banished to a cave. Before she could do so, one of the objects of her ire appeared on her doorstep, more food in hand. Beatrice could scarcely contain her anger as she took in the sight of the older woman. "Come in." She kept her voice frosty.

The smile on Mrs. Tisdale's face fell. "Good morning, Your Grace."

Beatrice didn't bother to correct her, only stood aside to let her pass. The words she'd been mulling over the last couple of days rolled around her head, and she wasn't sure where to start. "Over thirty years ago, I played with a boy I thought was an angel in the woods," she began, closing the door after Mrs. Tisdale.

The housekeeper's shoulders lifted despite the weight of the basket in her arms. She sucked in an audible breath but didn't speak.

"My parents accused me of being insane after I told them about him," Beatrice continued. "I don't know if they shared that bit of news with you. I was quite the embarrassment of my family for years afterward and was thought to be mad."

"I'm sorry to hear that," Mrs. Tisdale replied.

"I was subjected to humiliating tests from doctors to determine my sanity. I don't recommend anyone undergo such things, let alone a child of nine." She hadn't intended to tell the housekeeper that part. "I know now that I was correct about who and what I saw. Not about the angel, but about the boy I played with as a child." It was difficult to keep her voice steady. Hurt and anger at the injustice she'd been subjected to returned, and if she wasn't careful, she might take that out on Mrs. Tisdale. "I'm certain you already know who I'm speaking about," she continued. Mrs. Tisdale's eyes grew to the size of saucers.

"Beatrice."

Leo's voice had both of them turning their heads. He'd entered the foyer without either of them noticing, footsteps silenced by a pair of slippers. His wings lay flat against his back, the tops visible over his shoulders. "Hello, Ann," he said wearily.

"What are you doing here?" Mrs. Tisdale demanded.

"I brought him home," Beatrice replied firmly before Leo could reply.

The housekeeper looked at each in turn, as if she

didn't believe what she was seeing. She turned a beseeching gaze to Beatrice. "Your Grace, you cannot do anything to this poor lad. He has no one in the world to care for him and of course, no one can learn of his existence. Could you imagine what …"

"I could imagine." Beatrice wasn't sure which terrible thing Mrs. Tisdale spoke of. She chose her next words carefully, not wanting to scare of the other woman before she could learn why she had hidden Leo as she did. "His secret is safe with me, and he is safe in this house. Why did you want him to stay in a cave? There must have been somewhere else suitable that would have been more comfortable."

"There wasn't room in our house for someone of his size, and there was the risk you or someone in the village who isn't in on his secret would find out. We didn't think you would *stay* here!" Mrs. Tisdale exclaimed. Tears filled her eyes. Grabbing Leo's arm with her free hand, she said, "He's the closest I have to a son since my Bobby died. He's given us a reason to get up in the morning. I know the beach wasn't ideal, but it was the safest place I could think of on such short notice." To Leo, she added, "I'm so sorry, lovey. Are you being treated well by the duchess?"

"I'm not a …" Leo gave her a look that asked her to be quiet. Funny how she could read that in his pupil-less black eyes after so little time together.

"I'm well, Ann," Leo replied. "I promise. You did what you thought was best under the circumstances. I'm grateful to the duchess for her understanding and kindness throughout this."

His acknowledgement shouldn't have rankled her as it did, making her feel like the other aristocratic wives who treated acts of kindness and charity as a means to feel important. She had never been comfortable having stories printed about her donations to homes for unmarried mothers or volunteering with the Royal Society for the Prevention of Cruelty to Animals. It always felt exploitative and performative. There had been a personal reason for her seeking out Leo, to prove to herself that she wasn't mad, in addition to making sure a sentient person used to ordinary comforts could return home. God knew Clifford House had enough space for the two of them.

Besides that, Beatrice wasn't a duchess anymore.

"Leo is welcome to stay here as long as he likes," Beatrice said firmly. "His secret is also safe with me. I won't breathe a word of his existence outside the village."

"There are a few of us who have helped him through the years," Mrs. Tisdale explained. "Some of the newcomers to the village don't know, and it's best they never find out for Leo's safety. Do not speak of him outside the house."

A village like this likely defined a newcomer as someone whose family settled there a bare forty years ago. In some ways, rural folks weren't that dissimilar to the aristocracy. "Of course, I wouldn't," Beatrice promised.

Leo wrestled the basket from Mrs. Tisdale. "Let me take this."

Beatrice had forgotten all about the food delivery. "Have you not checked the beach the last couple of days?" she asked. Had she not noticed Leo's absence?

"I did. I left a basket there yesterday when I found the cave empty. I thought Leo might have taken a walk."

Where would he walk, exactly? Beatrice was likely to notice a giant bird and lion man striding around her property. Perhaps Mrs. Tisdale was getting muddle-headed in her old age. She opened her mouth to argue, then closed it when Leo gave her a warning look with a small shake of his head.

"So, there's still food in the cave," she said tiredly. That was bound to attract wildlife.

"I'll have that taken care of," Mrs. Tisdale replied.

"Is there anywhere in the village I can buy some?" Beatrice asked. "I don't have access to a steam cab or ornithopter or anything at the moment, so I would have to be able to walk there."

"There's a general store about a mile away. The Herefordshire airfield gets some supplies sometimes, too, if you're looking for a newspaper. Do you drive or pilot, Your Grace?" Mrs. Tisdale's voice was pitched higher, reminding Beatrice of a child who knew they were in trouble and was trying to distract an irritated parent by changing the subject.

"I can do both, although the duke kept the ornithopter in the divorce." Probably to show it off to Katherine, his new fiancée. Reginald hadn't been one for shuttling himself around town, preferring to hire a pilot or driver. "Thank you for the food and directions, Mrs. Tisdale. That will be all."

The housekeeper said her goodbyes and hugged Leo. She offered an odd half-curtsy to Beatrice, straightening halfway through as if she finally remembered that Beatrice was no longer a duchess.

Beatrice closed the door behind her and leaned against it with a sigh.

"You didn't have to be rude to her, you know." There was a stoniness to Leo's voice she hadn't heard before.

The remark immediately set Beatrice's teeth on edge. "She didn't have to leave you alone outside."

"She and Harold have done a great deal for me. They did what they thought was best, and I didn't suffer while I was there." Leo turned away and walked down the corridor, the basket still in his hand. Without turning his head, he added, "They didn't know what else to do. I had nowhere else to go. There are too many new people in the village who can't know about me."

Beatrice followed him into the kitchen. He unpacked the basket, placing waxed paper-wrapped bundles and a bottle of milk in the icebox. His wings twitched as he put everything away, and she thought he was probably taking his time to avoid looking at her. She wasn't sure how to make things right with him. "I'm sorry."

"Do you know what for?" He still didn't turn around, only looked through the nearest window at the empty garden. The glass was lightly misted with raindrops. Another fog had started to form.

"Meddling without knowing the circumstances," Beatrice replied dully. She wasn't ashamed of standing up for him exactly; she knew she should have done so more gently. It was a trait she'd been criticized for most of her life.

He finally turned around. His black eyes fixed on her, and his lips set in a thin line. "I accept your apology. Going forward, let me handle Ann and Harold."

"I will," she promised.

"Good."

"Is there anything else I should know about? What other toes should I avoid stepping on?"

"That's all I can think about when it comes to them. Oh, and don't mention their late son unless they've brought him up already."

"That's just good manners." Catching his raised brow, Beatrice added, "I am capable of following social conventions. I did so almost perfectly for twenty years." Thinking of the divorce coinciding with her twentieth marriage anniversary, she quickly added, "Almost twenty years."

"Until your divorce," Leo deduced.

"Yes." He made it sound as if it had been her choice. "It was Reginald's decision, so it was his divorce."

"What happened?" His eyes widened, as if he'd surprised himself by asking that. "Now it's my turn to apologize."

"It's fine. Half of London knows anyway and I'm certain the news has spread to the other half by now. I married Reginald at nineteen because it was high time for me to get out of my parents' hair and he needed a wife. We got on well enough for most of that. Last year he decided he needed to change his life, starting with me. To his credit, this time his bride-to-be has reached the age of majority." She pulled out a chair at the long table where a small army of servants had once prepared feasts and heavily plunked into it. Her blue skirt settled around her, still creased from being folded away in her trunk.

Leo's reply was incredulous. "He divorced you for someone else?"

"It's customary for dukes to merely maintain a mistress instead of marry them, but yes, he did." Taking a deep, shaky breath, she continued. "Katherine can give him heirs. I couldn't."

She'd never admitted that to anyone. Reginald hadn't even mentioned it during the divorce proceedings, only telling her in private when she demanded to know why he wanted to end their marriage after so many years. Beatrice was no longer useful to him.

He didn't reply.

She looked down at the tabletop, scarred from years of chopping and dicing on its surface. Chair legs scraped against the floor as he pulled one out next to her. To her mortification, tears sprang to her eyes. She patted her skirt pockets for a handkerchief and came up empty. An involuntary sob escaped her and she covered her eyes with her palms, unable to meet Leo's gaze. She had never cried about the divorce in front of anyone. She'd screamed at Reginald, scolded her solicitor, and snapped at acquaintances who tried to pry into their business. She hadn't let herself cry, to let herself show weakness in front of others in the face of the ultimate humiliation. Now she was doing it in front of someone she barely knew, whose life had been magnitudes more difficult than hers had ever been, even with the turn it had taken thanks to Reginald.

"You must have loved him," Leo remarked.

Her breath stilled as she mulled over the words. Clearing her throat, she said, "We got on well enough but we didn't love each other the way you might expect. We each had duties and I failed to fulfill mine."

"You may not have had the problem."

A mirthless laugh escaped her. "I know that but try telling that to a duke. I didn't even particularly *want* children."

That admission marked another first for her: voicing aloud her lack of maternal inclination. There was never a question about her not having children if she was capable of it. It was her duty as a married woman.

"Then why marry him?"

"It's what daughters of viscounts do. You marry well, hopefully above your station, and oversee your husband's household. You have children, at least one of them male, preferably two. An heir and a spare. If you're very lucky, childbirth won't kill you and if it does, your husband will find another viscount's daughter to marry after his mourning period has ended. Did you know a widowed man is only expected to be in mourning for six months, but a widowed woman two years?" She forced herself to look at him. His gaze was fixed on her, his expression otherwise betrayed nothing. "I don't know why I said that. I'm just angry about it. Reginald and I had a companionable relationship. He kept his affairs as discreet as he could. I was satisfied with companionable and discreet. Evidently, he was not." She sniffled.

Leo withdrew a handkerchief from his trousers pocket and held it out to her.

"Thank you."

"You're welcome. Thank you for telling me that. It explains a great deal."

"I wish I had happier stories for you. And what do you mean by that?"

He hesitated before answering. "You're not what I was expecting."

"You weren't expecting to meet me at all."

"No, but if I had, I would have expected a duchess to be less …" He fumbled for words.

"Rude? Abrasive?"

"Caring, I think."

She stared at him, agog. "Not an hour ago you scolded me for speaking to Mrs. Tisdale as I did."

"I think your words were well-intentioned. You insisted on my returning to the house with you. I've noticed that you haven't been eating much since I arrived, saving food for me."

"You were hardly eating yourself!"

"Because I wanted to make sure you didn't go hungry!"

Beatrice sagged against the chair and crossed her arms. She was ready to retort that he had been stuck outside for days and deserved food more, but didn't want their conversation to devolve into a full-fledged argument about who was more considerate. A smile crept across her face. Giggling, she said, "This is a ridiculous thing to argue over."

"I don't think we're arguing."

"It definitely counts." She dabbed at her eyes again.

Leo watched her.

"Do you want your handkerchief back?"

"It isn't important."

Beatrice carefully folded it anyway before stashing it in her pocket. Rising, she crossed the room and walked to the icebox. Lifting the lid, she peered inside. "What did Mrs. Tisdale bring us?" Almost everything was wrapped in waxed paper or cloth.

"Roasted chicken and beef, some cheese. There's a loaf of bread in there, too."

"Do you eat chicken?"

"Why wouldn't I?"

She turned around. He had a grin on his face, the first time she'd seen him with one. Like he had made a joke and she couldn't figure out the punchline. "You're part bird."

"Thank you for noticing. You're a full-blooded mammal and you eat beef, do you not?"

"I think they're sweet-looking creatures, but that's a good point. I just didn't think gryphons would eat other birds."

"I'm not entirely avian." As if to illustrate his point, his tail thumped against the floor. "Have you spent a great deal of time considering gryphon diets?"

"No, but until a few days ago I was convinced you were an angel."

He closed his eyes and tilted his head back, probably thinking about how to counter that. "You've spent time … you know, it's not worth the argument."

"This isn't an argument, it's a discussion. There are ready-made sandwiches here, too." She lifted the wrapping on one. "Tomato and cheese, even!"

His eyes opened.

"That's how we met. I had a tomato and cheese sandwich in my pocket that I shared with you, remember?"

He nodded. "I do."

"Let's have one." Without waiting for a rejoinder, she cut it in half and returned to the table.

CHAPTER 8

BEATRICE PROWLED through the parts of Clifford House she'd left unexplored since her return, needing to move but not wanting to go outside in the rain. Strains of piano music drifted through the house, as they had since she and Leo shared a tomato sandwich. When she thought about it now, she felt a little embarrassed, both at the suggestion in the first place and at her breaking down in front of him. He'd been nice about it, but it had to have been awkward.

Clifford House was largely absent of the comforts she was accustomed to in London. The electricity was scarce, used only in the kitchen and foyer as far as Beatrice could tell, although the appliances were still badly out of date. Most of the gaslamps worked when she twisted their switches, their lights were dim, making her glad she'd stashed a flameless candle in her skirt pocket. Some of the rooms were empty, the furniture probably having been sold off by her parents. Others were mostly untouched except for sheets covering the furnishings. There was an odor of dust in the air, especially in the east wing, making her sneeze a handful of times.

She hadn't been allowed in most of the rooms as a child. Her mother had insisted on keeping them as they were maintained by her own father and grandparents, and further back up the family tree. There was little belonging to Beatrice's parents or brother—no portraits or personal effects, nothing to suggest that they had once used this place as a retreat from the city. They hadn't returned after Beatrice spoke about playing with Leo. Her brother, Walter, hadn't put up a fuss when the house was left to her in their mother's will. On the rare occasion he'd spoken of Clifford House, he said the place was too depressing to spend time in, with nothing in the way of amusements in the village.

What a waste of a house.

The piano music grew louder as she traveled to the west wing, where her father's study and a library had been located. She found both intact, although the only personal effects in the study were stacks of dusty ledgers with figures written in both of her parents' hands. Clifford House once had a working farm, with plots of land parceled out to tenants. It looked like parts of the property had been sold off piece by piece, with the last sale occurring two years after her father's death. She'd died in her sleep not long after. Walter had died in a carriage accident a year later. He'd been kind to Beatrice, although he never believed her stories about the angel she'd played with. Walter was the person who set up her marriage with Reginald. As Beatrice told Leo, theirs wasn't a love match, but they had been friends. Beatrice knew what to expect in that kind of marriage and didn't let herself be too hurt when Reginald took up with his first mistress five years into their marriage.

First mistress that she'd known about, she mentally corrected herself. She didn't believe he waited that long before his first indiscretion.

She was delighted to find the library untouched, the shelves that stretched from floor to ceiling still filled with books. When she switched on a wall-mounted gas lamp, she saw the room was free from dust, the old velvet draperies recently shaken out, the rugs underfoot clean. There was a small upright piano in the corner of the room, an instrument she had forgotten about. When she raised the fallboard and pressed a key, the muffled twang that came out sent a shudder down her spine. If an out of tune piano affected her this much, she could only imagine how it would bother someone who could actually play. She dragged her fingertips over the books' spines, slightly disappointed to see most of the titles were related to agriculture and housekeeping. A few shelves down she found leather-bound works of Shakespeare and Elizabeth Barrett Browning, Tennyson and Dickens, the Brontë sisters and Ann Radcliffe. She plucked *The Tenant of Wildfell Hall* from a shelf and made a beeline for a green velvet-covered chaise. She remembered the chaise. It had been the focal point of the room, something she'd played on as a child when she sneaked into the library. It was an impractical piece of furniture that stood out in the staid library like a single hothouse flower, and as she draped herself over it, she thought this had to be the only thing she was actually pleased to own in the house.

She glanced at the bookshelves again.

The books were important too, surely. Some of them, at least. Beatrice had little use for anything about agriculture. Or Shakespeare, for that matter.

The piano ceased. A few minutes later, Leo's footsteps strode along the corridor, and he stepped into the room. "You've discovered the library."

Beatrice straightened. With her finger marking her

place in the novel, she looked up. "Would you believe I wasn't allowed to come in here when I was a girl?"

"Yes, but only because everything you've told me of your life is tragic." His voice was light despite the gravity of the statement.

She couldn't bring herself to be put out by that remark, not after she'd poured her heart out to him earlier. "So is yours. You've been raised by people of a different species and your existence is secret."

"And yours is scandalized through no fault of your own." He crossed the room to the chaise and looked at the end where her feet were propped, then gave a pointed look to her.

With an exaggerated sigh, she shifted position so her back was against the end of the chaise and her knees bent. Entirely improper, but who was there to care? "I didn't even tell you about what happened after I told my parents that I played with you," Beatrice said.

His eyes widened. The air in the room suddenly felt less buoyant. She immediately regretted her words. He hadn't even told her more about his life, clearly didn't trust her to open up yet. Leo must think her to be yet another selfish aristocrat. "What happened?" he asked.

She shook her head. "Never mind. Forget I said anything."

"*Beatrice.*"

There was an authoritative note in his voice that shouldn't have had the power to send a shiver of pleasure coursing through her but did. Hoping he didn't notice, she said, "Leo." Now it was her turn to arch an eyebrow at him. "Forget I said anything. It was a long time ago and I'm fine now."

"What did your parents do to you?"

She had the notion that if she told Leo what happened

all those years ago, he would be outraged on her behalf and she might cry again. "They didn't believe me when I said I played with an angel and I had to see a doctor for treatment." Her words came out in a tumbled rush.

"What kind of treatment? They didn't send you to an asylum, did they?"

"How do you know what an asylum is?"

"I do read a lot. Just because I don't travel doesn't mean I don't have a working knowledge of the world outside the village." His voice grew softer. "They *did* send you. The other day—you asked if I'd had children and if I'd send one to such a place."

She squeezed her eyes shut. Shame and anger formed a lump in her throat, and it took a few seconds before she could speak again. "It was only for a couple of days to scare me out of my delusions. Most of my treatment was at home from doctors my parents hired."

"Do you want to talk about it?"

Yes. No. "The suffering of the patients was immense," she said. She felt sick speaking about her trip to the asylum, how one of the doctors taking her on the tour had said that this was what happened to little girls who believed in imaginary friends. "I think I've forced myself to forget much of it. I heard screams from one of the rooms when we walked through the corridor like nothing else I've heard before or since. It was a sound of pure terror and pain. I still don't know what they did to that patient."

He didn't press further.

Beatrice tried to relax, to force her rapidly beating heart to resume a normal speed. Her leg slid down the chaise into Leo's lap. "Damn." She shifted, legs tangling in her skirt.

"It's fine. I took your seat, after all." Leo gave no intention that he intended on moving to another spot.

Beatrice thought she didn't want him to. He was a solid, reassuring presence she hadn't known she wanted until now.

If Beatrice kicked away the skirt's fabric to free her legs, she'd probably end up kicking Leo or forcing him off the chaise, and she found she didn't want to do that. As embarrassed as she was about unloading her pent-up memories and feelings to him, she liked having him close.

I hope I haven't scared him away.

He didn't move, only looked at her with an inscrutable expression. His black eyes were fixed on her legs, bent at the knees in a feeble attempt to give him more space. Even though they were covered by her skirt save for her stocking-clad feet, heat suffused through her at his perusal. Sitting next to him like this felt oddly natural, the kind of amiable feeling she'd never shared with her husband.

Leo shifted, his wings brushing against the back of the chaise.

"Sorry," Beatrice said, her voice breathier than she was expecting. She started to move to give him more space, only stopping when Leo put a hand on her knee.

"It's all right," he said. "They just get in the way occasionally. And there's the mess from molting. I apologize in advance for any feathers left behind." He looked over his shoulder ruefully.

Beatrice remembered the feathers found in the music room. "Are you losing them because of the changing seasons?"

Leo hesitated before replying. "Yes, and other reasons."

Alarm flared in her. Stiffening, she set aside her book. "Are you sick?"

"No. It's stress. That can cause excessive molting."

She was about to ask why he was experiencing stress,

thought better of it, and said, "It's because of me." It wasn't a question.

"Not because of *you*, exactly, but the change in my living conditions. Which have been rectified," he quickly added. "You're a lovely and very caring woman. I wasn't expecting a duchess to be so accommodating."

His compliment warmed her to her soul, and she realized she couldn't remember the last time anyone paid her one. Still, there was one thing he said that rankled her. "I already told you …"

"That you're not a duchess anymore," Leo finished for her. "You have the bearing for it, you know. Very regal. Your subjects must miss you."

"Duchesses don't have subjects. Kings and queens do."

"Well, you have the bearing of a queen."

Beatrice's breath caught. For a second, she thought she might cry. As it was, tears had already formed in her eyes that fought to fall when she blinked them back. It took a moment for her to find her voice. "Thank you."

"Why are you crying? Have I said something wrong?"

"No! Not at all. I'm just … people don't say nice things to me that often, is all. Usually, it's something about speaking out of turn." She gave him what she hoped was a wry smile. "I've never grown out of doing that."

Leo's response was unexpectedly earnest. "You shouldn't have to."

She would take that as a compliment, and the words warmed her to her soul. For a fleeting second, she wondered what would have happened had her family believed her when she told them about Leo or if she had returned to Clifford House even once in the years since she was a girl. What if she and Leo had been allowed to be friends? How would the course of their lives have changed? "Unfortunately, the rest of society doesn't agree with you. The expectations of a duchess are very strict and I didn't always meet them, as Reginald liked to point out." She nearly clapped her hand over her mouth. "I didn't mean to bring him up. I don't want to discuss him."

"Understandable." Taking care not to scrape her with his claw, his thumb brushed the top of her foot, a gesture Beatrice wasn't sure he intended but she appreciated.

To her surprise, another bolt of heat coursed through her, and she felt his touch as acutely as if her feet weren't covered in stockings. Part of her wondered what the pads of his furry fingers and thumbs felt like. Were they considered paws? The digits looked too human-shaped for her to tell.

His thumb dipped lower, gently massaging her instep.

Before she could stop herself, a moan of pleasure escaped her throat.

Leo paused. He had a hesitant look on his face, like he couldn't believe what he had just done.

Beatrice didn't want him to stop. "That feels nice," she said. Her voice trembled.

Leo blinked. He must have noticed. His reply came out in a low growl that shouldn't have had Beatrice's skin tingling yet did. "You deserve that." He pressed a little harder on her instep, thumb sliding under her foot to stroke there.

It should have tickled, yet didn't. Beatrice was torn between leaning into him to kiss him and pulling away altogether. She didn't deserve this kind of nice treatment, especially from someone who had been hidden away from the world. It wasn't just the status she'd married into; she'd had an inordinate amount of privilege for a woman. While she couldn't vote, she could travel freely, she could own property. She could be seen in public without being viewed as a freak of nature or put on display like a zoo animal, a certain fate for Leo should his existence ever be known. She'd been raised by her family, her own species. Leo deserved so much more, and she couldn't give any of that to him. She pulled away, putting her feet on the floor. Hurt flashed across Leo's face, an expression she forced herself to ignore. Looking away, she said, "I'm sorry. I have to go."

Without a backward glance, she bolted from the library.

CHAPTER 9

GUILT GNAWED at Beatrice for the rest of the day, lingering into the evening. She changed into her night clothes even though she knew sleep would likely be elusive.

She and Leo had shared an awkward supper, neither of them speaking other than to ask the other to pass the pepper. Her thoughts tumbled around her head, each one clambering to be spoken aloud, yet she had no idea how to present them. How did one explain feeling inferior and alone to someone shut away for his own safety without sounding like a petulant child? How could she accept kindness from him knowing the inequality in their stations?

Beatrice paced the length of her bedroom. Her nightgown swirled around her knees, and an old wrapper she remembered her mother using was around her shoulders. Clifford House's coal stores were empty and the room's fireplace didn't have any wood or kindling, so moving around kept her at least a little warm. Still, she wished she could finally get a decent night's sleep.

She was unsure of the time when she strode from her

bedroom, through the darkened house to the west wing. When she checked the music room, she found it empty and the gas lamps switched off. Stupid, she chastised herself. Of course, Leo wasn't playing. She would have heard him. Should she disturb him if he was sleeping? The selfish part of her demanded that she go to his room, knock on his door, and explain how she felt until he understood. The rational part of her urged her to leave him alone, it was the middle of the night for God's sake, and her time would be better spent trying to get some rest so she would have the energy to form an explanation in the morning, and...

Leo appeared in front of her, a flameless candle held aloft. Its light flickered shadows across his avian face, which would have been frightening had he not had his customary look of concern already written on it. "Why are you skulking about?"

She straightened. Her heart thundered against her ribs so hard she thought he might be able to hear it, although she couldn't tell if it was because she was startled or because Leo was wearing pajama bottoms and a robe, belted closed Briefly, the notion that he might be as disconcerted to see her in her nightwear crossed her mind. "I couldn't sleep. Did I wake you?"

Leo hesitated. "No."

Her chest grew tight. "Were you thinking about earlier today? How I muddled it all up?"

He looked affronted at the idea. "Yes, but not how you muddled it up. You have a very nice foot and ankle, at least what I could see of it."

The heat that had coursed through Beatrice earlier returned, temporarily making her mouth dry. How could the discussion of her foot bring about such a reaction? She felt a blush creep across her cheeks. "I've ... I've not been complimented on that before."

"I suppose there's a first time for everything."

What other first times awaited them? Another wave of heat washed over her as the selfish part of her resurfaced, wondering what he looked like under his night clothes. How would his lips taste? How would his skin feel under her hands? Where did his feathers end and fur begin?

"You're shivering," Leo said. "I have a fire going in my room. You could join me, if you like."

The possibility of sharing a warm room with Leo was irresistible. Beatrice's reply was an automatic, "Yes."

He smiled, teeth and fangs flashing white in the light of the flameless candle. "Good."

She followed him through the corridor to the west wing, footsteps muffled by the thick carpet underneath. Clutching her wrapper tighter around her shoulders, she wished she thought to bring slippers before seeking him out.

To her relief, his room was toasty warm, the heat enveloping her as soon as they walked in. The fireplace was alight, cheerful flames welcoming, highlighting the … Beatrice blinked. There was a giant nest on the floor. She turned shocked eyes to Leo, whose expression had gone sheepish. "My word. What is this?" she breathed. He'd mentioned he had a nest, but she hadn't been expecting this.

"This is my one indulgence."

The nest was huge, surrounded by tree branches and twigs, its sides extended almost to knee height. When Beatrice peered inside, she saw a mangled mattress, split apart, its sides lining the wood bits. It was piled high with blankets and bedsheets in an untidy tangle that looked strangely inviting. Half a dozen pillows were arranged at one end. "How on earth did you think I wouldn't have noticed this if I looked in this room when I arrived?"

"Oh, that. The door was locked when I was banished

to the beach. Ann and I thought you wouldn't bother with the west wing anyway, since it was used only for guests when your family summered here. And if you did, you'd assume some village children let themselves in to play."

The room was bereft of furniture save for a wardrobe and small table where an ewer rested. She'd been picturing warming herself in a chair before the fire while she and Leo talked about her lack of social graces, but there wasn't a spot to do that here other than his nest. It *did* look cozy. Beatrice had never been one for camping or other strenuous outdoor activities, but she supposed she could be talked into such a thing if she could rest in a giant nest after.

"You're not upset about the mattress, are you?" Leo asked.

"No. How did you do it?"

He held his hands. His shiny black claws winked in the firelight.

Beatrice's breath caught at the reminder that he was a predator. Or could be one, if he wanted to be.

"I also used a knife," he admitted sheepishly. "Gryphons traditionally don't use mattresses in their nests." He held out his hand in invitation. "You're welcome to join me. I have no nefarious intentions, I assure you."

Beatrice didn't know whether to be disappointed or relieved at the lack of anything nefarious. She stepped over its barrier, taking care not to disturb the twigs, then kneeled down on the mattress. As he'd promised, it was warm. "This is lovely."

Leo followed her, the mattress dipping under his weight. He sat next to her, then reached for a nearby pillow to fluff it. His wings folded against his back as he settled in. "Traditionally, gryphons live outside, but you've seen how I cope with the elements. Ann talked about building a little cabin for me on the estate grounds, but she had no idea how she would get that past you should you return."

The mention of Mrs. Tisdale set Beatrice's teeth on edge. "So, she thought it best you risk it in the main house." Catching his bemused look, she quickly added, "I'm not upset at all. I'm glad we met and that you're real after all these years. I wish you hadn't been treated as an afterthought and cast aside."

"I wasn't. The Tisdales are the last humans I know of who protected gryphons when we were still in this part of the world. They did their best."

Beatrice shifted so she was sitting. Stretching her legs out in front of her, she pulled a blanket over them. "I'm not convinced of that yet. Where are the rest of your kind?"

Leo hesitated before replying.

She hoped she hadn't said something wrong yet again.

When he spoke, there was a sad, wistful note to his voice. "They're all over Europe, what's left of them. We're a dying species. I have no means to reach out to where they may be, no way to explore. I can fly, but I certainly wouldn't be able to do that for long distances without someone noticing me."

"Where?" she pressed.

"Why? Do you think you could take me there?"

"Of course. I have the means to charter a dirigible if I want. Reginald didn't leave me destitute, although the stingy bastard certainly could have offered a better settlement to me, considering the reasons for the divorce."

He smiled. "I don't think I've ever heard you curse before."

"'Bastard' is hardly a curse. He deserves so much worse

from me. And I am *not* letting you derail the conversation. If you want to travel and find your family, I can finance it. You'll have to tell me which countries you want to go to, then I can charter a dirigible. You may have to hide below decks, and I am sorry for that, but …" Her voice trailed off.

Leo looked stricken.

"What is it?" she asked.

It took a few seconds for him to answer. "You were serious."

"Yes. Did you think I would joke about such a thing? I have no family left and I couldn't have children of my own. I know what it is to be alone in the world, too. Why wouldn't I help someone find their family if I have the means to do so?"

Leo lay back against the pillows and closed his eyes. He made a strange sound, like he was sniffling.

Beatrice wasn't sure gryphons could sniffle through their beaks.

When he spoke again, his voice was rough. "You would take me to Wales and Greece and the Ottoman Empire."

"Is that where they are? Yes. I've been to Wales before—lovely place, by the way—but other than that, I've only ever left England to visit France. I'd love to go with you."

"How does a duchess not leave England?"

Resentment at the question left a bitter taste in Beatrice's mouth. "I wished to travel, but Reginald forbade it. He said he had done enough traveling for both of us and the best place one could be was here."

"You are no longer a duchess, as you've never failed to remind me."

Beatrice grinned.

"You could travel now," he pointed out.

She lay down and rolled on her side to face him. "I

can, and I can do it with you, someone who *wants* to see the world. Have you ever left England?"

"No. My parents were the last of their kind here. I do remember them, although they passed when I was young. My father died shortly before we met in the woods, actually." Leo gave a rueful shake of his head. "He was a good man and I miss him very much. I used to wish he'd left England and taken me to another gryphon flock, but he was older when I was born, and age took him before he could make those arrangements. Both of us were too weak to fly there, and with the rise in air travel, I don't think it would have been possible to do so without someone seeing us and our ending up as zoo exhibits. So, I've stayed."

It was the most Leo had spoken of his earlier life since they met again. Pain and loneliness tinged his words.

"I'll take you, if you want. I mean it," Beatrice promised.

"It's a very generous offer that I'll accept. I've never been aboard a dirigible before." He reached for her hand, squeezing it. His palm was bald of feathers, the skin softer than she expected.

Beatrice laced her fingers through his, holding her breath for his reaction.

To her relief, he responded, claws lightly scraping the back of her hand when he relaxed in hers.

"You'll enjoy it, I think."

His eyes fixed on hers.

She found herself unable to look away. His eyes were so dark they didn't have irises, at least not ones her human vision could detect, yet she could still read him when she looked into them. There was a look of tenderness reflected there, something that sent a bolt of heat through her. She felt herself flush and wondered if he noticed. "When did you stop regretting being left in England?"

He looked away for a moment. His fingers tightening around hers. "There are a few reasons."

Beatrice's heart gave a squeeze. The selfish part of her wondered if it was her, but that was preposterous. They'd only reunited after a chance meeting thirty years ago. They hardly knew one another. Or did they? God knew she had told him things she'd never shared with anyone. He'd been equally forthcoming.

"You're one of them," he said. "I'm glad you're here. Well, it's *your* house, but I'm happy we've become friends."

She felt like giggling. As it was, a squeak of laughter escaped from her. Catching his quizzical look, she explained, "Sorry. I'm not in the habit of cuddling with my friends in nests. I like it," she quickly added when his expression didn't change. Just as she wasn't in the habit of holding hands with her friends. Nor did she want to kiss them the way she wanted to kiss Leo.

He shifted position, letting go of her hand to touch her hair, unbound and loose around her shoulders. "It looks like a crown."

She hadn't been expecting that. "My hair?"

"It's gold and silver. It's very pretty. I hope you know that."

The compliment warmed her to her toes, the first one she'd received in—she didn't want to think about it. A lump formed in her throat that she had to swallow before she could reply. "Thank you." As soon as she said the words, she was grateful that she hadn't laughed it off. The tears that had threatened her earlier returned. To her mortification, a few fell. "Sorry," she whispered hoarsely. "I'm usually not so emotional. Well, I am, but I'm not used to hearing nice things about my appearance these days, and …"

Leo kissed her.

The response Beatrice had flew away in her surprise. Her breath caught in her throat, taking half a second to return. Her body flooded with heat, heartbeat picking up its tempo against her ribs. She eagerly responded, shifting to get closer to him but he pulled away, breaking their contact.

Opening his eyes, he blinked, like he was as shocked as she was.

She didn't speak, and waited for him to collect his thoughts.

When he finally spoke after what felt like an interminable stretch of time, his voice was rough. "You're one of the reasons I don't regret staying here. I remembered you and the kindness you had for me, playing and sharing your food. I think…" He cleared his throat, maybe stalling for time. "I think part of me was waiting for you to return."

The admission floored Beatrice. For one of the first times in her life, she was speechless. Leo tucked a lock of hair behind her ear, trailing his fingers down her neck. A frisson of pleasure coursed down her spine, pooling between her legs at the contact. Closing her eyes, she leaned into the touch, only opening them at the sound of a wordless rumble escaping from him.

"What was that?" she whispered.

"Are you familiar with house cats?"

"Of course. Was that a purr?"

He grinned. "That happens when I'm very happy and comfortable." As if to emphasize his point, his tail peeked from beneath the blankets, the end tickling her hand.

On impulse, Beatrice stroked it, drawing an unexpected moan from him.

"That wasn't a purr," she pointed out.

His reply came through gritted teeth. "No, that was,

'now I know what it feels like if she touches my entire tail.' It felt very good."

Did that mean…? Beatrice didn't ask, not wanting to embarrass him. "Like when you touched my foot."

"You *do* have very nice feet," he replied wryly. "I like touching you, is all." He lowered his head and kissed her again, with more confidence this time, like he wasn't afraid she would pull away.

Determined to make sure he knew she wanted him to touch her, Beatrice shifted closer, her arm sliding over him in a clumsy embrace. When he gasped against her lips, she touched her tongue to his, noting with surprise how cool it was. Strange—no, *different*. She felt as hot as the fire that blazed in the hearth.

He responded again, tongue tangling with hers as another moan escaped him. Abruptly, he pulled away, his hold on her loosening. Disappointment filled Beatrice, and with it, a yearning ache to feel his bare skin against hers.

Leo cuddled her against his chest. His breath came rapidly, the rise and fall of his chest a testament to what he was feeling. "I need to slow down," he said, voice rough with desire.

"That's all right."

"I like you a great deal. I … I'm very attracted to you and there are a million things going through my head right now about what I'd like us to do." He paused, searching for words.

Beatrice held her breath, grateful he wasn't rejecting her.

"I never thought something like this might happen. I'm not ready for more yet." His arms tightened around her.

Beatrice understood. Part of her felt the same, having never experienced intimacy with anyone but her husband. This felt a little overwhelming.

"Will you still stay with me tonight?" he asked.

She couldn't believe he would ask such a thing. "Of course."

He pressed a kiss to the top of her head, arms tightening around her. "Thank you."

CHAPTER 10

Beatrice lay on her side, curled up next to him. She looked peaceful in sleep in the gray morning light peeking through the draperies, a few strands of hair falling over her forehead. Leo resisted the urge to brush them back from her face, unsure if she was a deep sleeper or not.

He wasn't, which was why he was awake now thanks to early morning birdsong. He'd never taken it, but he was certain if he tossed back half a bottle of laudanum he would still be roused by it. Whether it was a primal link to them thanks to his avian side or finely tuned feline hearing, he couldn't say.

Carefully stepping out of his nest, he noticed the fire burning low and banked its remaining logs to keep Beatrice warmer. Clifford House had a coal cellar and furnace, although it had been empty for years. Who would keep a supposedly unoccupied house stocked with coal? Leo had made do with the house's fireplaces since he moved into it when he was a young adult, but he doubted that would keep it warm enough should Beatrice decide to stay here permanently. His heart squeezed when he thought about her leaving. She'd not announced definite plans, but he couldn't see a reason for someone like her to stay in rural Herefordshire for too long, even if she had been divorced and disgraced in London.

Who would divorce such a lovely creature, anyway?

He glanced in the nest, where Beatrice still slept, oblivious to his absence. She was just as beautiful in sleep, unfettered with worry. Heat roiled through him at the memory of their kisses the night before, as innocent as they had been. Leo couldn't believe his own audacity in the library when he'd taken the liberty of touching her. Then later, when he invited her into his nest. It had felt oddly right to wake up next to her, like she belonged next to him. To the best of Leo's knowledge, gryphons didn't take mates the way other species were rumored to. He hadn't met any other preternatural creature in his life, but Ann had told him tales of werewolves and vampires passed down in her family through the ages. She believed they still existed and were hiding in plain sight. Some species had what she called fated mates they were destined to fall in love with and spend their lives together or forged permanent bonds with their chosen lover. It was a strange relief to Leo to know that he still had free will over his life and partner, if there was one for him.

There is.

Beatrice was the woman for him. He knew it in his bones. Just as he had suspected as much when they met as children, although he hadn't had the words for what he felt back then. At eleven years old, he'd only known that she was special to him, not just as his first playmate his own age. His *only* playmate, he recalled. He hadn't been permitted to play with the other children in the village for fear one of them might blurt something out when in the wrong company.

The icebox and larder hadn't been replenished yet, but there was enough food to tide them over until tomorrow morning. Beatrice didn't usually eat much to break her fast, but perhaps that was because she was used to servants preparing her meals. Leo made a note to ask her about that as he boiled tea and eggs. There was half a loaf of bread left and he sliced off a couple of pieces to toast them. As he did so, his black claws glinted in the weak sunlight that suddenly appeared through the kitchen windows, sharp and lethal. His digits were designed to catch prey unaware, not sweep along piano keys to coax out a sonata.

Or touch a human's delicate skin.

He cringed, thinking about what could have happened had he not put a stop to their... what was the word Ann once used? *Firkytoodling.* What a stupid term.

Heat surged in him at the memory of Beatrice's soft skin and quickened breaths, and with it, shame at his inability to follow through. He'd imagined what Beatrice looked like under her clothes for days, a dozen fantasies simultaneously running through his head, and when the opportunity arose, he froze. It wasn't just the state of his claws, although they were a factor.

He eyed the bread resting on a plate before him. Toasting it could wait while he took care of his claws.

Leo strode through the house to the bathroom once reserved for Clifford House's guests, largely unused since he moved in. It had been updated with pipes that offered running water and little else. This room didn't have electrical power, instead relying on a gas lamp that offered weak light. It was decorated with a feminine touch, tiled with pink-veined Italian marble, its long-disused tub finished with shiny brass fixtures. He ignored them for the oversized cabinet resting against the far wall, filled with an assortment of old beauty implements that had to have once belonged to Beatrice's mother or grandmother. Rifling through one of the many tiny little drawers, he found a dusty manicure set in a copper box. Inside, he found what he was looking for, a pair of nail scissors and a file. The scissors proved to be too small for his paws, and it took a few tries to hold them comfortably. A few moments later, his claws were neatly clipped to the tips of his fingers, a file run over the edges to remove any lingering sharpness.

He regarded his fingers with a critical eye under the dim gaslight. His fingers were still covered in tan fur, but aside from that, they looked almost human. If he could ignore that what was left of his nails were colored black, that is. Beatrice didn't seem to mind. Leo had never trimmed his claws like this before, and the sensation of his fingertips digging into his palms was novel as he walked back to the kitchen. To his surprise, he found Beatrice there, toasting the bread. "Good morning."

She smiled at him in return, the sunlight picking out the gold and silver in her hair. It reminded him of when he'd told her it looked like a crown the night before. It was pinned back in a knot at the base of her neck, the curls threatening to escape from its pins. She'd dressed in a simple white blouse and trousers that looked a little too big on her curvy frame. "Good morning to you, too. I see you've started breakfast." She barely concealed a yawn behind her hand before pouring the brewed tea into a pair of dainty porcelain cups.

"There are a few boiled eggs in the pot on the stove."

"I saw them. Can I have one? I'll leave the other four for you."

"Of course. You can have whatever you want." Why did it suddenly feel like a kaleidoscope of butterflies had taken flight in his stomach? He'd shown her his private nest and invited her to share it. He shouldn't be feeling like a besotted schoolboy at this point in their relationship.

"Thank you." She fished the eggs out of the copper pot on the stove, arranging them in a bowl. "The bread should be toasted soon."

Leo nodded.

"Are you surprised?" she asked.

"About what?"

"That I know my way around a kitchen."

"Not really," he lied.

"I was not the kind of useless duchess you might have read about," she chided him.

"I never assumed you were."

"But you did assume that women of—well, my station, I suppose—wouldn't have any domestic skills. You would be correct on a lot of those counts, but I can boil water and toast bread." She was babbling, which Leo couldn't remember her doing before. She was nervous, he realized.

"Is something wrong?" There. May as well nip that in the bud now.

She hesitated before replying. "Did I do something wrong last night?"

"What? No! I liked sleeping next to you. I liked waking up next to you. You looked so peaceful this morning and I didn't want to disturb you."

"No, it isn't that. I'm honored you let me see your nest. It was ..." She bit her lip in a becoming way that made him want to kiss her. "Look, I won't be offended if you, if you prefer gryphon women. I thought perhaps you wanted to spare my feelings ..." She trailed off.

Rejecting her. He hadn't done it out of a lack of attraction. "No, no, it wasn't you at all. I like you," he assured her. That had to be the understatement of the decade.

What he felt for her transcended friendship. He nodded at the table. "Sit down, Bea."

Her eyes widened.

"Did I misstep calling you that?"

"No, I've just never had a nickname before. I like it."

The reassurance bolstered Leo's confidence. "Then take a seat and I'll explain it to you."

"I can't. The bread will burn."

"I'll take care of the bread. I started breakfast, anyway."

Beatrice obediently sat at the table, watching as Leo prepared their plates. Their food remained untouched as they gathered their thoughts. "I like you very much."

"I thought you might not be attracted to me." Her voice was small, on the verge of breaking.

"Of course I am!"

She looked away for a few seconds before forming her next question. "I expected, I thought you and I would …" She sighed in frustration. "Engage in bed sport."

The clinical term shouldn't have been as funny as it was. Leo relaxed a little. "I wanted to. Believe me, I did."

"Why didn't you? Is it a compatibility issue?" She flushed pink as she said the words.

"No." If he'd been capable of it, Leo would have been blushing as well. "It's more of an experience issue, or lack of it."

Understanding dawned on her. "Oh! You've never … well, I guess there aren't any lady gryphons nearby."

His earlier relief gave way to embarrassment again. "It isn't a total lack of experience on my part. I was intimate with a human woman about fifteen years ago."

Her blond brows arched upward. "What?"

"She's a niece of Ann and Harold's. It was more to satisfy curiosity than anything, on both of our parts."

Beatrice's expression was unreadable.

"Anyway, it was a brief affair and she has since married and left Herefordshire. Ann and Harold don't know, nor does her husband, as far as I know. I'd prefer it remained that way. I think she would, too."

Beatrice made a twisting motion over her lips with her fingers, like a box's clasp being closed. "Your secret is safe with me."

"So, there's a distinct lack of experience there. I've also not brought anyone else to my nest, as I've told you. I was nervous, is all." It felt good to tell her that, to open up to her the way she had to him.

"So was I," she admitted.

"Why would *you* be nervous?"

She gave him a look that questioned his intelligence. "Because I was faithful to the husband my brother picked out for me and he couldn't be bothered to return the favor?"

Leo's paws curled into fists. He longed for the opportunity to pummel the bastard who made her feel like she was less than. "You're still young," he protested.

"I'm nearing forty."

"I'm already forty. It isn't a bad place to be. Neither is Herefordshire," he added wryly, hoping to lighten the mood a little.

She smiled. "I've already learned that. The Herefordshire part, at least. I'm still uncertain about the forty years old part." She finally reached for her tea and took a long drink.

It bothered him that she saw ageing as something bad, but he reminded himself that was unfamiliar with her aristocratic world outside of what he read in books and periodicals. Still, hope flared in him at her liking Herefordshire. Liking *him*. He reached for a piece of toast and helped himself to a couple of eggs. He'd left them to boil longer than he preferred when he decided to cut his claws, but they were still edible. Beatrice hadn't said anything about his nails yet. Maybe she would notice later. "I'm a little out of practice with my music," he remarked.

"Is this your way of telling me you want to perform a concert for me?"

"Yes. Playing piano is what I'm best at."

She arched a brow at him again. "Are you sure? You're a very good kisser."

A surge of desire coursed through him at her words. "I'll take the next opportunity I can to practice *that*."

CHAPTER 11

BEATRICE HAD BROUGHT *The Tenant of Wildfell Hall* with her, intending to read in case Leo opted to practice instead of play, but the novel was ignored. His paws easily swept across the keys, bringing to life pieces that had never been played on the instrument when her family visited Clifford House. To think he'd only had lessons from Ann Tisdale, yet was playing "La Campanella" and "Fantaisie-Impromptu" with a skill and passion she had never heard demonstrated until now, including the recitals held by Reginald's stuffy friends held in equally stuffy parlors.

He would never get a chance to play before a proper audience.

The realization made her sad. Setting aside her book, she caught Leo looking at her in a way that made that thought evaporate and her mouth dry. That was a come-hither look if she knew one.

"You're frowning," he said.

The statement reminded her of what she was mourning on his behalf. "Are you bothered that you can't perform a concert for the public?" she blurted.

He shrugged without taking his paws off the keys. "I would love to see and hear what kind of instruments are available to professionals, but I imagine I would come down with stage fright before performing. Doing it for you is different," he quickly clarified. "You won't criticize me."

"I think you play beautifully," she replied.

"That's the only accolade I need now."

She'd been trying to compliment him, yet he'd turned it around on her. "But don't you get lonely for the outside world? You know so much about it, I thought you might want to experience it."

That comment earned another shrug from him. "There's a decent chance I would end up captured and displayed in a circus, isn't there? Besides, what Ann and the other villagers know about me, what you've said about it, I don't feel like I'm missing a great deal. You don't seem especially happy with it, if I'm being honest."

"That's an astute observation. I have a lot more freedom here," she admitted.

"You weren't your husband's equal."

"No."

"We are here."

She liked how he said "we." She crossed the short distance between the chair setup to the piano, leaning in the curve. Its rosewood body was cool against her back through the thin material of her blouse, the vibrations from the keys gentle as Leo played. "What's this?" she asked. "I don't recognize it."

"'Intermezzo in A major. Opus 118. Brahms. You've probably heard it before."

"Maybe. I don't have a head for music other than you play beautifully."

Leo's paws slowed on the keyboard. Beatrice turned around to look at the strings and hammers depressed under his control. It was incredible that someone could manipulate such a random-looking assortment into producing music.

The hammers lifted as he released the pedals, the final notes of the opus evaporating. Leo closed the keyboard lid and rose. Beatrice didn't move, waiting for him to join her. He touched her hair, one of its pins loosening under his fingertips. "Can I take these out?" he asked.

Her answer was breathless. "Yes."

Heat roiled through Beatrice, her body flooding with a long-forgotten desire as he loosened her hair. The rational part of her brain reminded her that she might never have experienced something like this in the first place, that she was feeling true need for another for the first time in her life. Did it matter?

Leo's lips pressed against the side of her neck. *No, it doesn't matter.* His fangs lightly scraped against her skin, drawing a whimper from her. Both of them froze, but he didn't remove his hands from her waist. "Did that hurt?" he asked in a hoarse whisper.

Her legs nearly gave way from relief. She hadn't scared him off. "No, I want you to do that again, actually."

"I thought so, but …" He repeated the motion, lightly biting the sensitive spot under her ear.

"Leo, I promise I will tell you if I don't like what you're doing, just as you said you would tell me." She turned around so she could better see him, the piano digging into her back. There was a look on his face she had never seen before, open with longing. His black eyes glittered. If she had been able to see his pupils, she thought they would be huge from pent-up desire. Behind him, his wings quivered, white and gray feathers finely trembling.

Raising a paw, he ran the backs of his fingers along her cheek, down her neck to the small part of her throat that was exposed by her unbuttoned blouse. The light, gentle touch made her breath catch and goosebumps pop up along her skin. She slid her hands up his torso to his shoulders, the thin linen of his shirt hardly a barrier to the furred muscle it concealed, encouraging him to kiss her again, which he enthusiastically did. When his tongue touched hers, she mewled, a sound that encouraged him.

His paws scrabbled for her hips, pulling her body closer to his until she could feel the outline of his cock against her belly, a sensation that made her mouth go dry. He broke their kiss long enough so he could pin her with a heated gaze as he reached for her blouse's top button.

Beatrice nodded her assent at his silent question.

With shaking fingers, he unbuttoned her blouse, revealing a travel corset that she wore for practicality and comfort rather than seduction. Judging by the way his eyes widened, she didn't think he cared about the old cotton garment and its lack of lace or color, especially when he touched the exposed part of her chest with a reverence she'd never seen before. It wasn't until he reached for the first clasp on her corset that something was off about his paws, her mind taking a few seconds to register what she was seeing.

"What happened to your claws?" she asked. The black nails were almost gone, blunt and dull.

"I clipped and filed them." If he'd been capable of blushing through his feathers, she was certain he would. "I didn't want to risk hurting you if … if things came to this."

Understanding dawned on Beatrice. "You planned ahead."

He gave her a lopsided grin that sent heat pooling between her legs. "I was very hopeful."

She nearly blurted out that he could have had her last night in his nest before he clipped his claws, but refrained in time. He hadn't been ready then. "Thank you for thinking of me."

"I think about you all the time, Beatrice. I wondered what happened to you and why you didn't come back when we were children but from the first time I saw you again on the beach, I think I've …" He paused, as if fumbling for words. "I'm obsessed with you now."

His confession nearly brought tears to her eyes. She closed them for a moment, willing them away, not wanting to spoil this moment. Beatrice hadn't felt this close to anyone in her life, hadn't known she was missing this kind of synchronicity until now. *I've found my other half.* The thought was fleeting, but potent.

Leo was kissing her neck again before she could voice it, a distraction she couldn't ignore. Her fingers reached for his shirt, wanting to start undressing him as he'd done to her, but he stilled them, lightly holding her hands in his paws. "Do you think the music room is the best place to do this?" he asked shyly. There was an undercurrent of lust to his voice that made her shiver beneath the question.

Her voice came out in a rasp. "Why not? This is your favorite room in the house. It's where you feel most comfortable." Another thought struck her, and she felt like an idiot for not considering it earlier. "Is this an … um, is this an anatomy issue that has to be solved elsewhere?"

His eyes, glazed with desire, widened a little. "Why would the music room have something to do with anatomy?"

"I don't know."

"Have you thought about my anatomy?"

"Of course I have," she replied indignantly.

He bit back a smile.

"In fact, I'm thinking about it right now." She pushed a little against him, the hard outline of his cock pressing against her pelvis again, a motion that coaxed moans from each. "Do you require a certain kind of bed or position or what?"

He closed his eyes for a few seconds, a muscle ticking in his jaw. He looked like was trying not to laugh.

Beatrice took that as an encouraging sign.

He wasn't so nervous about making love to her. "The notion of taking you against the piano is a tantalizing one," he admitted.

"How so?" The teasing note slipped into her voice without her trying.

His next words came out in a rush, as if he hadn't had time to mull them over. "I imagine you would have to turn around as you were earlier, the lid closed and your palms against it as I took you from behind."

A strangled sound escaped Beatrice. "That sounds fun."

"It would be, except for our differences in height. You would need a stool to be comfortable. I'm not certain that the bench or chaise in the corner would be strong enough to withstand both our weight, and I would prefer that our first time not be on the floor rutting like animals." He straightened a little. "I may look like one, but …"

"You are *not* an animal."

"I would also prefer to reduce the risk of being discovered in a private moment by Ann or Harold, who I hate to bring up now but who have been entrusted with the house's care and come and go as they please."

Having one of the Tisdales walk in on them like that was the stuff of nightmares Beatrice hadn't considered. "So, shall this continue in my bed or your nest?"

"What is the lady's preference?"

She shook her head. "I don't care."

He considered her answer for a half-second. "My nest,

then." Without waiting for an answer, he picked her up and briskly strode for the corridor.

Beatrice had never been bodily picked up by a man before and found she liked it.

"I meant it when I said I would like to try this in the music room sometime." His walk was purposeful and deliberate, voice trembling with lust.

"You've thought about it, then?" She clutched at his shirt, linen bunching under her hands.

"Just as you've thought about our anatomy."

"Yours, mostly, and you haven't answered my question about compatibility."

"You didn't ask about that specifically, if you recall. The conversation was sidelined a little."

She held her breath as he jogged up the stairs with more grace than she was expecting.

"I also mentioned positions."

"You did, and that was nearly my undoing, so I'm pleased the subject was changed."

Once in his bedroom, he locked the door behind them before stepping into his nest. Gently, he set her down in the middle of it, on top of the unmade bedding before lying next to her. He kissed her with a slow tenderness that belied his earlier urgency but was no less intense.

She eagerly responded, letting him hold on to her as he rolled on his back, taking her with him.

"This," he said, voice a breathless whisper.

She tilted her head, waiting for him to elaborate.

His response was rough. "I want you here. I want to see you."

Beatrice thought she might combust and took a few seconds to gather herself. "Then that's how you will have me." Leaning down, she pressed her lips against his, his mouth opening in welcome.

This time, he didn't protest when she reached for his clothes with shaking fingers.

She helped him with hers, grateful she'd had the foresight to pick out a pair of plain trousers that morning. He fumbled with the clasps on her corset until its sides were pulled apart, baring her to him before she could finish helping him take off his own trousers. Leo stilled at the sight of her straddling his body, her skin pebbling in the cool air, nipples hardening under the heat of his gaze.

"You're really beautiful, Bea."

Tracing a finger down his bare chest, she marveled at the way the feathers on his shoulders gave way to fine tawny-colored fur that was darker near his trousers' waistband, the buttons unfastened but still on his body. His hips bucked a little against her, a pained expression crossing his face. "That feels good," he murmured.

"I want all of this to feel good for you."

"I think it will." He looked at his paw again, at the shortened claws. "I was more worried for you."

"There's that question about anatomy again."

He lightly pinched her nipple, drawing a squeal from her and sending a bolt of heat straight to her core. He looked shocked at his own audacity. "Did I hurt you?"

"No. I will tell you if you did. I liked it, actually." She leaned forward, bracing her hands on either side of his head. Shifting so his cock pressed against her, he moaned, grabbing her hips to encourage her to do it again. "It doesn't *feel* like there's going to be an issue with our anatomy."

"I just don't want to hurt you, is all." His voice was strained. Abruptly, he let her go. "If that continues, this will be over before it starts."

"You won't hurt me." She reached for his paw, guiding

it to her center. "Feel me here. I'm ready for you. You did this, Leo."

Hesitantly, he pressed one of his digits against her. Beatrice didn't try to hold back her moan, wanting to encourage him. Emboldened, he pushed it inside her, into her slick heat. A purr vibrated in his chest, his black eyes dropping to half-mast from wanting her. They fixed on her as he pushed a second finger inside her.

Beatrice's thighs screamed in protest from the angle she was straddling him in, a feeling she ignored as she lowered herself on his paw, wanting more of him to fill her. His breath was ragged and labored, his hips rising and falling in tandem with his fingers sliding in and out of her. Beatrice's body begged her to move faster, to make herself come against his paw, but in a valiant effort of self-control she forced herself to still.

So did Leo, who withdrew his hand and reached for his trousers instead. Beatrice helped him, sliding his clothes down his legs and pushing them away. His cock was heavy, pearlescent fluid at the tip, its fur lighter than the rest of his body. *No anatomy incompatibilities, then.* She felt like giggling in delight but knew it was likely to be unappreciated, well-intentioned it was.

He ran his paws down his length, the look on his face hungry as he watched Beatrice, like he was waiting for her reaction. Just as quickly, he let go. "Hair trigger," he muttered.

Her hand resting on his thigh, she asked, "May I?"

"Mind the hair trigger."

With a grin, she wrapped her hand around it, experimentally dragging it up and down his length. He groaned, lifting his hips as he did. Wanting him to feel good, she leaned down, prepared to take him in her mouth, but he put his hand on her head to stop her. "Remember what I said?"

She straightened. "Some other time?"

"Oh, God, yes. But not yet." He pulled her down for a kiss, both of them shifting so Beatrice could take him into her body.

She held her breath as she slid down on his length, taking her time as her body adjusted to the invasion, not letting it out until he was fully seated inside her. Beneath her, a shudder of pleasure coursed through Leo, his body straining below hers. He placed her hands on his chest, then his on her hips, as he slowly withdrew and pushed into her again. "That feels good," she bit out, which had to be the understatement of the year. It felt *amazing.* Beatrice matched him thrust for thrust, letting him set their rhythm. The first stirrings of an orgasm rose in her, just out of reach as Leo plunged into her over and over, his black eyes hooded and not leaving her face as he watched her reaction.

His speed increased, breath coming faster, a sign that he was close, too.

She wanted to finish together. She grabbed one of his paws, dragging it across her skin to her where their bodies joined. Leo immediately understood, pressing a finger against the bundle of nerves that begged for his attention. A harsh cry escaped her, a reaction that had Leo moving faster in and against her.

"*Yes,*" he growled.

That was all it took for Beatrice, whose climax exploded inside her with an intensity that pulled a near-scream from her throat. She hadn't meant for that to happen, not yet, not until Leo had found his pleasure, but his eyes were scrunched closed, mouth open and panting as he recklessly slammed into her body, groaning as he came.

Hot seed flooded her as his body vibrated beneath hers in his intense orgasm.

She didn't move or speak, waiting for him to do so first. Beatrice was still buzzing with pleasure despite feeling like she had been wrung out, all rational thought gone, replaced by warmth and belonging. It felt like she and Leo were the only two people in the world.

Still inside her, Leo opened his eyes. "*Beatrice.*"

"I'm still here."

He took her face in his hands, kissing her with a hungry desperation she wouldn't expect from someone who had to be tired and spent after what they had just done. "Stay here with me," he said against her lips.

"I will."

Leo pulled away just enough so their eyes could meet. "Always."

Beatrice kissed him again. "Yes."

CHAPTER 12

Iᴛ ᴡᴀs the second time Leo woke up next to Beatrice, a positive sign. *Another* positive sign, he reminded himself, which had to be an understatement, considering all that had transpired between them. They'd had an early supper together with the last bits of meat and cheese from the icebox, the bread heels shared between them, before returning to his nest to make love again.

He was awake alone again. But the trepidation and nervousness he'd had the day before was gone, replaced with a euphoria and happiness he'd never thought he would get to experience. The fact that the kitchen was nearly out of food didn't bother him as he made his way toward it on bare feet. His dressing gown—a castoff from Harold, lengthened with extra material and with cutouts for his wings— was loosely wrapped around his waist. There were a couple of eggs, he remembered. Eggs and tea. It wasn't much. Ann and Harold hadn't been by with food deliveries in a few days. Not for the first time, he wished Beatrice's family had opted not to dismantle Clifford House's old chicken coop and tear up the vegetable gardens. He had descended the stairs when he saw Ann walking toward the kitchen.

She stared at him in shock. "Leo! Why aren't you dressed?"

He had to have been a small child the last time she saw him in bedroom attire. He couldn't remember the last time he'd this kind of awkwardness in his life. "It's rather early," he replied cagily.

She narrowed her eyes at him. "Where's Her Grace?"

If she was here, Beatrice would correct the housekeeper immediately. "Mrs. Duff is still sleeping."

Ann didn't immediately reply. Slowly, her expression shifted into something resembling shock. "Where is Mrs. Duff sleeping?"

"In a bed." His answer came out more aggressively than he intended. It was technically the truth. His nest was a bed.

Understanding dawned on Ann. She pressed a hand to her mouth. "Oh, Leo. Firkytoodling?"

He checked the belt on his dressing gown, noting it was still secured. He still felt exposed despite its cover. He shifted his weight from one foot to another, trying vainly not to fidget. His wings fluttered of their own accord, a sign Ann would recognize as nervous. *You are a grown man,* he reminded himself. *Beatrice is an adult, too. We've done nothing wrong.* "For the love of all things holy, please do not ever use that term again."

To his pleasant surprise, Ann sighed. "All right. As long as she can keep your secret, I suppose."

He exhaled in relief. "Thank you for your blessing."

Ann pinched the bridge of her nose between her fingers. "What about your heart?"

"My heart is fine. Better than fine. I love her." He'd never voiced the words before, let alone to Beatrice, but as he said them, he knew they were true. A brand new, different kind of anxiety seized him—what if Beatrice didn't feel the same way? He knew her well enough to know that she wouldn't sleep with him for a lark, that she cared about him in her way, but love was something completely different. She had been burned by it before.

Ann's expression softened. "That's good."

"I never expected to have that," he admitted.

"Nor did I." Something in his expression must have betrayed his hurt reaction, because she quickly added, "We did our best with you, but there are some things human guardians can't provide for a gryphon, including other gryphons to mate with."

"Please don't say 'mate with' again."

She waved her hand in dismissal. "Fine. I was just about to leave, anyway. I left some food in the icebox, and I left a telegram for Beatrice on the table. It arrived last night."

"Telegram?"

"Yes, it was sent to the airfield office all the way from London."

A cold chill formed around Leo's heart. "I'll let her know. Thank you for bringing everything over."

"You're welcome. Do you think Her Gr—Mrs. Duff would be amenable to building a new chicken coop? There's so much land on the estate that's going to waste. The Millers down the road would love a chance to rent some of it for their cows, too. At least they mentioned that before they went on holiday. They'll be returning soon."

The Millers knew about Leo, so their renting a few acres of the Clifford House property wouldn't pose a risk to his safety. If his mind wasn't clouded about what could be in that telegram, he would bring the subject up with Beatrice right away. The Millers could be their friends;

they could be normal couples who had supper at each other's homes, if she wasn't about to be summoned back to London.

Remain calm. It's entirely possible the telegram is just a note from a friend.

But hadn't Beatrice mentioned not having true friends in London? *An acquaintance then or perhaps her divorce solicitor.*

"Leo?" Ann said. He blinked, realizing she had said his name more than once while he'd been gripped by the possibility of her leaving.

He nodded. "Yes, of course."

"You'll speak to Mrs. Duff about the Millers' cows?"

"Right away, Ann."

"Thank you." Brightening, she adjusted the buttons on her coat, a light one she had had as long as Leo could remember. "The weather is finally warming up. You and Mrs. Duff should take a stroll around the estate today. Put on trousers first," she quickly added.

His dressing gown came nearly to his ankles and covered his wrists, so there wasn't anything on display, yet he still bristled internally at the suggestion. "Of course. Thank you again for bringing everything over." After he bade Ann good-bye at the servants' door in the kitchen, he immediately made a beeline for the table, where a large cream-colored envelope rested in the center. It was addressed to the Duchess of Bewdley, Clifford House. Picking it up, he saw it was sealed with a blob of red wax sloppily applied to the envelope flap, easily lifting in his hands. His heart in his throat, he considered opening it and reading the missive. The envelope was already open. Beatrice would never know. It might put his mind at ease that she wasn't leaving him, and if it was a summons back to London—he squeezed his eyes shut. He didn't want to think about that.

He dropped the telegram like it had scalded him.

No, he would not invade Beatrice's privacy like that. What would he do if the message ordered her to leave? Throw it in the fireplace? Another telegram was sure to arrive in a few days. What if it had good news for her? Besides that, Leo wanted Beatrice to know the choices she had before her, wanted her to choose him of her own free will. Only a day before he'd been grateful to have his. He wouldn't be able to live with himself if he took that away from her. With a sigh, he set about making a pot of tea. He wedged the envelope between a pair of cups on a tray and carried everything back to his bedroom.

Beatrice was awake when he returned, the nest's blankets drawn around her. "Bless you," she said, eyeing the tray in his hands.

Leo set the tray on the highboy and poured cups for each of them. "Ann stopped by with some more provisions."

"I'll have to tell her thank you when she comes back. I wanted to ask you something that completely left me yesterday."

His face heated. "We were distracted."

"Yes, and a pleasant distraction that was." She cleared her throat. "Um, the compatibility we have. Does that extend to reproductive compatibility?"

It took a couple of seconds for Leo to understand the question. "Oh! No, I don't think so. Gryphons can only have children with other gryphons."

"Oh, thank God." She leaned back against the pillows. "I've never wanted to have children, although I always assumed I would have to. I suppose that's a terrible thing for a woman to admit, but it's the truth."

He shook his head. "No, not terrible." Leo had never entertained fantasies of fatherhood, although it wasn't entirely due to the lack of gryphons. It had never truly appealed to him.

"That is a huge relief to hear."

She gave him a smile that made his insides quiver and other parts stiffen. He hated having to ignore his physical reactions in favor of delivering the rest of his news. "Ann brought something else. A telegram for you." He handed a cup and the envelope to her before stepping into the nest himself.

She wrinkled her nose, staring at the envelope. "Where on earth would one send and receive a telegram here?"

"The airfield has services for the locals."

"Ah." She set aside her tea and lifted the envelope's flap, removing a folded sheet of paper. Her eyebrows knit together as she scanned the words, mouth turning down in anger. Her voice held an undercurrent of rage. "I'll be damned. It's from Reginald. He's requested that I return to London at my earliest convenience."

Leo nearly dropped his cup. His wings trembled. "Oh?"

Her eyes darted back and forth over the telegram's words again. "I'll have to go. If I don't, I'm certain he'll come here and we cannot have that," she said darkly. Crumpling it in her fist, she looked like she wanted to throw the thing in the fireplace and feed its burning embers. For some reason, that reminded Leo of Ann's telling him about the spring weather, her suggestion to take a walk in the sunshine. Would that happen today?

"I'll make arrangements this morning," Beatrice said.

"You're leaving?"

She pinned him with a stare. "Yes. And I'll return, I promise."

"What does Reginald want?" he couldn't help but ask.

Beatrice smoothed out the crumpled telegram and

handed it to him. "Just to talk to me by any means necessary."

Her balling up the paper had caused the telegram's printed gold logo to flake. Beneath it were a few terse sentences from Reginald, ordering her to return to London for a meeting between the two of them. *I WILL COME TO CLIFFORD HOUSE IF I DO NOT RECEIVE A PROMPT RESPONSE* read the final line.

"He divorced me and he's still trying to control my life." Beatrice's words came out in an enraged hiss. She rose and stepped out of the nest. "I'll arrange to leave at once."

"Today?" Leo said weakly.

She nodded. "The sooner I go to London, the sooner I can come back to Clifford House."

I love you. Don't go. The words stuck in Leo's throat. As much as he wanted to say them, he resisted. His timing couldn't be worse. Saying them now would only muddy the waters further, perhaps even come across as manipulative. Beatrice was a free woman, with the right to make her own choices unimpeded at last.

"I'll be here," Leo promised.

She gave him a tight smile. "I should hope so."

BEATRICE LEANED over the railing of the dirigible's passenger deck, watching at London's Vauxhall Airfield came into view. The scarred boards vibrated beneath her feet as the craft's anchor was lowered, steam issuing from its bottom. She clung to the railing, knowing what was about to happen next as the dirigible began its rough descent to the waiting dock below. A few yards away, a young couple shrieked when they nearly tumbled to the deck.

She'd booked passage on the first dirigible making a stop in Herefordshire, a cheap one that only offered outdoor seating. It had been two days since she'd received the summons from Reginald, only a few hours since she'd kissed Leo goodbye. Her heart ached at the memory of his devastated expression, trying to keep up a cheerful front when she left Clifford House. The fact that she hadn't even brought a change of clothes with her wasn't a consolation to him. Although given the dust and grime present on the dirigible's exposed deck, she now regretted not bringing anything to change into for her trip back to Herefordshire.

Midday at the airfield meant that it was full of people. Beatrice wove her way through the crowd, stopping at the flight office to check the return schedule. To her relief, she could go back at half-six and hopefully return to Clifford House in the late evening. It was unfortunate that she would have to spend the day in London, but at least she would have some time to research private dirigibles to charter. She hadn't forgotten her promise to Leo to look for his relatives around Europe. Perhaps he would even get to fly alongside the dirigible when the skies were quiet.

Beatrice hailed a steam cab to take her to the town-house she'd once shared with Reginald, the house she'd been promised in the divorce. The driver looked at her askance from his perch when the cab stopped in front of its drive. "Are you certain this is the correct place?" he asked.

She did not look like a viscount's daughter or a former duchess. Her hair had all but fallen out of its style and she was certain there had to be dark circles beneath her eyes from sleeplessness and stress. Beatrice wore trousers instead of a skirt, the fabric streaked with dust from the journey. Sometime between her arrival in Herefordshire and return to London, her coat had lost two buttons. Her hat had never recovered from being soaked in the rain the first night in the village and its feathers drooped, the material all but ruined.

"Yes," she replied curtly, handing a few coins to him.

"You want me to wait for you?"

He thought she'd be thrown out for daring to step foot on the property. With a sigh, she said, "No, thank you. I'm expected. You may leave now."

With a shrug, the driver pulled at the cab's levers and the vehicle clattered away, steam and smoke issuing from its vents.

Beatrice took a deep breath and looked up at the townhouse, fortifying herself. Nothing about it had changed in her absence. The same draperies were arranged behind the windows, the door had the same tarnished brass fittings, something she once intended to repair. She rang the bell and waited.

A moment later, a liveried man she didn't recognize opened the door. He was young, perhaps in his early twenties, his uniform a touch too large. "Yes?"

Had Reginald hired a new butler? "I'm here to see the duke."

"Is the duke expecting you?"

She removed the telegram from her pocket and held it out. "I'm his former wife. He asked me to come here."

The butler's brows lifted. "Oh, yes. The duke mentioned that. Please come in." He stepped aside to allow Beatrice room to pass. "May I take your coat?"

"No, thank you. I'm certain this will be quick."

The butler looked dubious at her answer but didn't refute it. "Please wait …"

"In the front parlor," Beatrice finished for him.

Without waiting for a reply, she let herself into the

front parlor, settling on a blue velvet chair. She'd picked them out herself years ago, back when decorating the house was her full-time hobby. Idly, she wondered if Reginald had started erasing her presence from the rest of it, if Katherine, his new fiancée, would be changing things to her tastes after they married.

The copper clock on the wall ticked seconds, its hands at two minutes to one o'clock. She waited for the little metallic cuckoo bird to pop out from behind its door to announce the time. God, how Reginald had hated that clock. Too noisy and uncouth, he'd declared. Cuckoo clocks were out of fashion and in poor taste. Beatrice waited until the cuckoo returned to its hidey-hole, then rose, crossing the room and taking it off the wall. It would look nice in the kitchen at Clifford House.

A few moments later, Reginald walked in the room, blanching at the sight of Beatrice. She leaned back against the chair's overstuffed back. "I don't have long," she said by way of greeting.

He was dressed like he was going to church. The gray suit was familiar, but the light blue shirt looked new. Reginald didn't usually wear colors. That had to be Katherine's influence. He didn't offer a perfunctory smile, and Beatrice wasn't about to pretend that she was glad to see him, either. "Good afternoon, Beatrice." His voice was steady, but there was an undercurrent of exhaustion to it. She peered at him, noticing for the first time that there were hollows under his eyes, his cheeks a little thinner beneath his waxed moustache. Had he lost weight?

"Why am I here, Reginald?" she demanded.

He eyed the clock in her lap. "What are you doing with that?"

"I've always liked it. I'm taking it home."

He flinched at the mention of 'home.' "I wasn't

expecting you to come back so soon. Shall I call for tea? Trenton would be happy to bring it."

"Is that your new butler? What happened to Mrs. Adams?" Beatrice cast a critical eye around the parlor, noting for the first time that the space was dusty. The housekeeper had always been so fastidious in her work.

"Katherine did not care for Mrs. Adams and made that evident."

Beatrice arched a brow. "She sacked her? Have you two already married? That was faster than I expected."

Reginald looked pained at the question. "No."

"How can a mere fiancée sack a long-serving and faithful employee?"

"It was more of a mutual decision. Mrs. Adams has found another post and will not return no matter how much I've asked. *Beatrice.*" His voice turned beseeching, like a small child who was desperate for his parents not to refuse what he wanted.

She gave a silent prayer of thanks to whoever was responsible for her not having children with this man. "What is it, Reginald?"

"Katherine. We're no longer engaged."

The news wasn't as much of a surprise to Beatrice as it should have been. "Did she remember that she's young enough to be your daughter?"

Reginald looked wounded at the question. Beatrice hadn't known he was capable of being hurt. "In a manner of speaking, yes. She said that when she ended our engagement."

"But not before sacking your staff."

"Yes, she's upended things in a way I can't put back together."

"No." Her voice was sharp enough to have Reginald's eyes widening in surprise. "You did this. *You* upended your own life and mine. Let me guess. You've ordered me back here to convince me to return to you, haven't you?" She'd wondered about that on the flight, mulling over the possible reasons the bastard wanted to see her again. A reconciliation attempt made sense. She hadn't dared mention it to Leo, not wanting to worry him further.

God, but do I miss him already.

"I know I haven't treated you well. I had hoped—I thought we could work through this together, make a new start of it." Reginald said. There was a practiced sadness in his voice, as if he had rehearsed this speech, wanting to tug at her heartstrings. Inauthentic. His hands were clasped tightly together, something she had never seen him do before.

Fury rose in Beatrice. For half a second, she considered whipping the clock at his head to fully drive home her rage, but it would be a waste of a perfectly charming cuckoo clock. She would probably end up arrested if she did that, anyway. "Are you fucking joking?" she seethed.

Reginald blanched. "You don't use that kind of language, Beatrice."

"I do now, since you divorced me to marry a younger woman! I should have started using it when you kept mistresses without telling me. Yes, I know all about them and so did everyone else in society!" She rose and paced the length of the room, feeling like an enraged animal captured in a cage, waiting for the first chance to strike and bite. "So, I ask you again. Are you fucking joking? Why would I reconcile with you?"

"I'm lonely. I'm lost without you. You made this house a home."

His words still sounded hollow, reciting a list of reasons Beatrice should make up with him. "I see divorced men receive little more respect than divorced women in this fucking city," she snapped.

"Beatrice—"

She shook her head. "No. Never. Our divorce is finalized and official."

"Is there someone else?"

She hadn't been expecting that question. She debated telling him no, but that would invite further pleading for her to return. *I don't want to lie about Leo.* She might not be able to share that he wasn't human, but she did need to make it clear to Reginald that they would never, ever reconcile. "Yes. I love him."

God damn it, I should have told Leo that before I left.

Reginald looked like he'd been slapped in the face. "What?"

"Do you think no man would ever want me? You're dead wrong. He adores me as much as I adore him." She hoped that was true. "And after today, I never want to see you again." Hugging the clock to her chest, she stomped out of the room, nearly crashing into Trenton, who held a tray in his gloved hands. Without another word, she walked out of the house into the spring sunshine.

CHAPTER 13

How was it possible for a day to feel so endless?

Beatrice had promised to return to him as soon as she could, perhaps even that night if she could find a flight that had Herefordshire on its route. She'd left that morning, taken to the airfield in Harold's carriage. It only provided a small measure of relief to Leo that she didn't have any luggage with her, nor had she worn anything that might appeal to her former husband. He remembered her telling him about how much the duke hated it when she wore trousers, and Beatrice had worn them on her journey.

What if she remembered how much she liked modern conveniences in London? Clifford House and the village barely had electricity, let alone things like steam-powered vehicles, shops that sold anything anyone could possibly want, and telephones. Leo had never seen a telephone, but he had read about them in the periodicals Ann and Harold received in the post. What if Beatrice landed at the airfield there, took a ride on an Underground train or popped into a shop that sold more than one kind of jam, and realized how little Clifford House and Rainfield had to offer.

How little *Leo* had to offer. He couldn't even court her properly.

It was nearing half-ten, the sun having long ago set. The house was silent save for the faint ticking of a grandfather clock in the library, audible to ears as sensitive as Leo's. He'd had a glass of brandy from a bottle with a faded label he found in the study, hoping to soothe his nerves; unfortunately, the taste was so off-putting he poured half of it down the sink. He tried to read, picking up Beatrice's copy of *The Tenant of Wildfell Hall* that she'd forgotten in the music room, but he couldn't bring himself to read more than the first few sentences before his mind started to wander.

So, he practiced piano, fingers skimming over the keyboard, playing the same pieces he'd entertained Beatrice with the night before. His face grew hot and the front of his trousers uncomfortably tight when he relived those moments, his promises to her about what he wanted to do. Would they ever get that chance?

He closed his eyes, hands stilling. *I miss her. I love her.*

An unfamiliar buzzing sounded, loud enough to shake the house's windows. "What the hell is that?" Leo muttered. His words swallowed by the noise. Dashing to the window, he saw a huge dark shape descending on Clifford House's unused field, the one the Millers wanted to rent. Sharpening his focus, he picked out the shape of … he squinted. A floating boat?

A dirigible.

He'd never seen one up close before, just the occasional craft soaring overhead. "Beatrice," he murmured. This must be her doing. Hope flared in him, bright as a pyrotechnic, and he dashed through the house to the servants' door in the kitchen. The rumbling stopped before he reached the dirigible. Part of him said this was crazy, to stay inside in case this wasn't Beatrice's doing, but the possibility of it being hers was too much to resist. A pair of giant lamps mounted on either side of the dirigible's bow flared to life, flames licking the inside of what looked like glass cylinders. Amazing. The sight of the lights wasn't as amazing as Beatrice, striding down a gangplank to the ground, a triumphant grin on her beautiful face. Without another thought, Leo dashed for her.

She threw herself into his arms. "I'm so glad to be back."

"I thought you might not return." The words slipped out before he could stop himself.

Beatrice raised her head from his chest. Her hair was windblown, cheeks pink. She smelled of dust and tea, underlaid by a scent that had to be unique to London. Her eyes were wide with surprise. "Why on earth would you think that?

He tightened his hold on her. "Because I can't offer to you what the city has."

"The city has nothing I want."

"What about Reginald?"

Beatrice rolled her eyes, the casual action belied by the angry set of her jaw at the sound of his name. "What about him? His fiancée left him. He can't be seen in public without a wife, and when he brought that up, I essentially told him …" She hesitated.

Leo felt his own ire rise. "He wanted *what*?" he growled.

"Shall we come down now?" The voice was female, coming from the dirigible's upper deck. A slim figure waited, lit up from behind by the deck's lamps, her features nearly indistinguishable aside from wisps of red hair. She held a baby on her hip.

Beatrice turned her head over her shoulder. "One

more moment, Arabella. Thank you." To Leo, she said, "You'll never believe what I found in London. A private dirigible to charter! The couple who owns it, well, they're a little like us. He's a …"

"Reginald wanted you back," Leo said. "And you told him what, exactly?" Jealousy, hot, unfamiliar, and unwelcome, rose like bile, leaving a sour taste in his mouth.

"I essentially told him to go fuck himself." Beatrice gave him a quizzical look, as if she couldn't believe she would have any other answer for her former husband.

Leo bit back a gale of laughter as relief poured through him at her explanation.

"You can't possibly think I would want to go back to Reginald. Not when I have you. I love you, Leo. I've never loved anyone else like this before."

He hadn't known how much he wanted to hear those words until she said them. He'd had every intention of saying them to her himself, yet to hear them healed a piece of his soul that he hadn't known was scarred. "I love you, too," he breathed into her hair. He pressed a kiss to the top of her head, hair tickling his beak.

"Your Grace?" the woman called Arabella called from the dirigible. There was a lilt to her voice, like she was saying it to needle Beatrice.

It worked. "I'm not a duchess anymore," Beatrice called back.

"You're a queen," Leo murmured into her ear.

Beatrice smiled up at him, haloed by the dirigible's lights. She broke their embrace, grabbing his hand to guide him to the dirigible. "You'll have to meet Arabella and Xavier Kinnon, the dirigible's operators. Their daughter, too. Charlotte is very sweet for someone who can't speak in sentences yet. They'll stay with us for a few days while we figure out an itinerary for our journey to find other gryphons. Arabella is a very experienced aviator." They walked up the gangplank.

Arabella's baby had red hair, the same as her mother. From an enclosed glass box on the deck, a sandy-haired man stepped out, shyly waving at Leo. "This is the first time I've met a gryphon," Arabella announced. The baby's eyes slowly closed. Wasn't it terribly late for a baby to still be awake? Could a baby even sleep when aboard a flying machine?

At least they weren't scared of Leo or surprised by his appearance. "You said they were like me," Leo said. Curiosity had him scanning the Kinnons' faces for traces of feathers or fur, but they looked like regular humans.

"My other form is a dragon," Xavier offered. "We think Charlotte may be a shifter when she's older, too."

Leo had not been expecting such an answer. "I didn't know there were still dragons about."

"I think I'm the last one." There was a trace of pain in Xavier's voice at the admission.

"I understand that. There aren't a lot of my kind left, either," Leo replied. To Beatrice, he asked, "How did this come together? How did you find out about Mr. Kinnon's dragon half?"

"'Xavier' is fine." He collected Charlotte from her mother's arms. "We'll get you in bed soon," he murmured to the baby.

"I found them when I was looking to charter a dirigible," Beatrice explained. "Their advertisement at the Vauxhall airfield said they could handle all things and passengers unusual and strange. They know how to get visas for other countries. Their dirigible has a secure and very comfortable hold for guests who need to stay out of sight or sunlight."

"Why would someone need to stay out of sunlight?" Leo asked.

Charlotte fussed against Xavier's shoulder. "We have met werewolves on our travels. As soon as we told Beatrice about that when she asked about our experience, she said we sounded like a good fit for chartering," Xavier said.

"Xavier also gave her a demonstration of his dragon side below deck," Arabella added.

Beatrice nodded, eyes shining with wonder. "It was incredible."

Charlotte wiggled in her father's arms, then began to cry. "She needs to get back to sleep," he reported.

"Let's go inside. You can take the viscountess's suite," Beatrice announced. Lacing her fingers through Leo's, they walked down the gangplank, Xavier holding Charlotte and Arabella with a satchel over her shoulder.

"Do you still want to go?" Beatrice whispered to Leo.

"I'd love nothing more," he replied. "As long as I'm with you."

BONUS SHORT STORY!

"Unexpected Mate" is a Magic & Mechanicals short story originally written for a charity anthology that has gone out of print. It takes readers back to the Roseheath Barony in Scotland, run by the werewolves introduced in *Wolf's Lady*, the first Magic & Mechanicals book. Enjoy!

UNEXPECTED MATE

June 1890, Scottish Highlands

Calum Campbell didn't have to look at an almanac to know the full moon was close, but he didn't want to be impolite to his mother who held hers out to him, like she had to remind her son why he was so out of sorts. *The British Almanac and Companion* was something she ordered and looked forward to receiving in the post every year.

"You're drooling." Fiona Campbell's voice was stern. Calum touched his lips and to his mortification, found saliva there. He unceremoniously wiped it away with his shirtsleeve. Her expression was reminiscent of the time he had dragged a pair of rabbits into the house after his first shift, even though he'd brought them home for supper, trying to do something nice for his mother. "I did *not* raise you in a barn."

"I'm half animal. I'm certain I can be forgiven for forgetting my manners once in a while. And I don't think this qualifies as forgetting my manners, on account of being half an animal."

Fiona narrowed her eyes. "That's hardly an excuse. Half animal still means you're half human. And you get the human part from me, and *I* know not to go off wandering when the full moon is near."

"If I don't return in time, I'll still be able to shift in private. There will be no one anywhere in the vicinity of Ben Nevis. I won't run, I won't howl, I'll only turn into a wolf as long as I'm compelled to, perhaps eat a deer, then wait out the rest of the night until I'm human again." His mother opened her mouth to argue, but Calum continued. "And that's *if* I don't return in time. Which I will."

Fiona narrowed her eyes at him. When she didn't immediately offer a rejoinder, Calum knew he had won the argument. It wasn't as if she could keep him from leaving the barony; his shifter blood gave him an inhuman strength and speed, not that he would ever use it against her. Or anyone, he supposed. The only time he was remotely aggressive was when he was in his wolf form and game animals were unfortunate enough to cross his path.

Fiona finally looked away, her gaze focusing on a small painting of a field, completed by Calum's late father long before he was born. "I don't see why the baron couldn't go himself," she muttered.

"The baron is a devoted husband and insists on staying with Lady MacAulay and their new baby," Calum reminded her. The baroness of Roseheath had recently delivered their third child, a little brother to a pair of twins. While she was being assisted by Mrs. Tuplin, the barony manor's long-serving housekeeper, Lord MacAulay still preferred to stay close to his wife. Besides that, Calum considered it an honor to be asked to complete the task ahead of him.

Water. All he had to do was fetch a couple of bottles of water from the River Nevis and bring them home. Calum was even given leave to take the barony's newly acquired ornithopter for the journey. The allure of a trip in the beautiful flying machine was too strong to ignore, impending full moon be damned.

"I don't see why the baron can't wait until after the full moon to send you," Fiona protested. Calum barely suppressed a sigh.

"The baron predicts storms over the next few weeks. He said excessive rain could taint the river water." Calum had been in the baron's workshop when he'd made the comment, pointing to one of his barometers. Lord MacAulay had several throughout his home. "It's very important that he gets this water for his next experiment. He wants to compare if there is a difference between the water here and sourced from elsewhere when used in lubricant for his prosthetic limbs manufacturing. He…" Calum trailed off as his mother's eyes glazed over. She had never been one for discussion of the sciences, a passion he and the baron shared. "Never mind," he mumbled, looking away.

"Fine."

Calum's gaze snapped back to Fiona. "You're not going to argue about this?"

"I want to, but there's no point. You're going to take off in that flying deathtrap whether I like it or not." Her voice took on a beseeching note, rare for her. "Promise me you'll be back in time for the full moon. I don't want to think about what could happen if you're trapped on the mountain."

Excitement surged in him. "I'll be fine," Calum promised.

Louise was decidedly not fine.

Fighting back a scream of frustration, she looked at her tent, her possessions visible through the open flap. The logical part of her said she should wash up at the river's shore, then try to get some sleep before setting out for civilization in the morning. The impulsive part of her—the reason she was in this mess to begin with—told her to grit her teeth through the pain shooting through her wrist, pack up everything, and start the long walk back to Fort William. She let out an angry sigh. If the damn horse she had rented hadn't thrown her, she wouldn't be in this position now. "Stupid animal," she said aloud.

Her only answer was the sound of the River Nevis rushing past her.

Stupid animal, and stupid Louise for insisting she could handle riding such a creature through a mountainside. Who the hell rode horses through mountains? Why hadn't she listened to anyone who said this journey to Ben Nevis was a bad idea? And now she had an injured wrist that was probably broken, defeating the entire purpose of the trip. She was supposed to be drawing, creating a portfolio so dazzling she was certain she could land an exhibition at a gallery in Aberdeen, perhaps even Edinburgh.

What if she could never hold a pencil again? A shudder coursed through her despite the summer heat. She would *not* let herself think of such a thing.

With her uninjured wrist, she picked a pebble from the ground and tossed it as hard as she could into the river, the rushing water too loud to hear it drop.

A squeaking sound overhead had her forgetting her pain for a few seconds. "Insects," she muttered. "That's all I need to make this worse, a swarm of flying insects."

What kind of noisy insect was active at night? She

racked her brain, coming up with mosquitoes as the noise grew louder. Looking up, she saw a giant metallic-skinned creature, wings flapping awkwardly at its sides. She shrieked in surprise, a very unladylike, "Fuck!" escaping her as she scrambled to her feet. Cradling her injured wrist, she took a few steps back in the tent's direction, then stopped as her vision registered what was above her: an ornithopter, its wings brass-colored and glowing in the light offered by the setting sun. And it was shifting downward, preparing to land.

Oh, no. Louise was alone, with little more than sharpened pencils to defend herself with. She frantically looked around, as if the mountain or the river could tell her what to do next, coming up empty.

The craft landed about ten yards from her tent. Louise stilled as a tall figure stepped out of its basket, wearing a bowler hat that definitely looked masculine. She glanced at the river again, trying to guess if she could make it across without drowning. *Fool, your wrist is broken,* she chided herself.

"Good evening." The interloper's voice was warm, sending an unexpected wave of heat roiling through her.

Ignoring it, she focused on him. "What are you doing here?" she asked, not bothering to hide the hostility in her tone. Better for him to think she was rude and leave her alone.

This close, she could see he looked to be perhaps twenty-five, her age, with glowing whiskey-colored eyes, the pupils dilated. *Glowing?* She blinked, clearing her vision, and his eyes now looked normal. His lips were full beneath an aquiline nose, skin tanned from the summer sun. His flight jacket was a little too large, hanging past his wrists, a pair of flight goggles pulled down around his neck to rest against his chest. Full lips turned up in a slight smile that she supposed was to be reassuring. Damn him, it worked. He was an attractive man.

"It's unusual to see people setting up camp here, and I wanted to be certain you're all right," he replied. Removing his hat to reveal a head of short, tousled dark hair, his head tilted to the side as he studied her. "Have we met before?"

Now it was her turn to scrutinize him. She would have remembered their meeting. "I don't think so."

He looked at her again, gaze warm. Giving her a small bow, he said, "I'm Calum Campbell of Roseheath."

The name meant nothing to her, but the bow oddly did. "Louise Bell. I'm from Bowhill."

"You're a long way from home."

"So are you," she retorted, although she had no idea where Roseheath was.

"I'll be returning there shortly. I just have to get some water first." Spying her injured hand, still held against her, his eyes widened in concern. "What happened?"

"It's nothing."

"Your wrist is turning purple!"

"It is not." She looked down at her arm, noting with horror that it was indeed turning an alarming shade of purple. Damn it, she should have tried harder to hide it, but that was impossible when she was wearing a blouse with sleeves that didn't meet her wrists. "It's fine," she lied, remembering how only moments ago she'd silently berated herself for not being fine.

"It's sprained, if not broken." He thumbed back at the ornithopter. "Do you want some help?"

She hadn't expected that. "You can set a broken bone?"

Calum's reply was patient, like she should expect that all ornithopters were equipped with medical supplies. "Of course." Without waiting for her reply, he turned away and walked back to his ornithopter, returning with a small red-painted wooden box. As if her body could detect that help was near, her wrist's ache seemed to increase.

"Can we sit there?" he asked, nodding his head at the old tablecloth she had spread on the ground. Her sketch-book lay unopened on the yellowed linen, a mockery of her inability to draw.

She nodded, hoping she wasn't about to make yet another huge mistake.

Once settled on the tablecloth, he flipped open the box's lid and withdrew a flameless candle. As its tiny light sprung to life, she noticed that it was rapidly getting dark, the sun sinking behind the mountainside. *Oh, my God, I'm about to be stuck on a mountain with a total stranger!*

"May I?" he asked, pointing to her wrist.

Yes. No. She held it out to him, wincing at the movement.

With the candle in one hand for light, Calum gently inspected her wrist, prodding it with a light touch. Louise sucked in a harsh breath. "I think your wrist is sprained," he announced.

That news should have provided a small measure of relief, but Louise was too distracted by the feel of his fingers on her. The heat she felt the first time she looked at him returned, hotter this time, an intense magnetic pull. She wondered if she had met him before, then quickly dismissed the thought. She would remember that attrac-tion, not to mention his eyes turning glowing in the light of the flameless candle.

Calum raised his head, his eyes a lighter shade of gold, almost animalistic. The expression on his face was still serene, although there was a set to his jaw that hadn't been there before.

I would love to draw him. Louise had never been drawn to portraiture before, focusing on landscapes around Scotland and England. Perhaps it was time to expand her subjects.

He removed a rolled-up bandage from the box. "I don't think it needs a splint," he reported. His voice had shifted, its warm velvet tone growing deeper, almost a growl. It should have been more alarming to her than it was, yet she found herself oddly intrigued. Sparks danced up her arm where he touched her, the sensation so intense that her heart skipped a beat. There was something so familiar about him, like she had known him for years, even though she was certain they had never met in her life.

Just to be sure, she blurted out, "Have you ever been to Bowhill? Maybe we met there once."

He shook his head, then started to wrap her wrist. His hands seemed to tremble in the dim light. "Never been."

"London? I was there recently, for a gallery exhibition for my cousin. Well, second cousin, to be precise. Bit of a wanker, but he did put on a good show." She was babbling. Why was she babbling? The next thing she knew, she would be telling him about the performance art her second cousin, Julian, got into the local newspapers.

"I've never been to London. I've never left Scotland, to be honest with you." He pinned the bandage in place. "It'll be good as new in a few days."

She flexed her fingers. Already, she missed the feel of his skin against hers. The compressions certainly reduced the pain. "Thank you."

"It was my pleasure." His gaze searched her face. A sudden wave of self-consciousness washed over her at his scrutiny. "How did you get here?"

She hadn't been expecting that question, although she probably should have. "I've been on a camping trip for a few days. I haven't been to the mountains since I was a girl and wanted to get some sketches for a new series of paintings."

"And you walked here yourself, with all your supplies?" He thumbed at her tent.

Embarrassment welled in her, and Louise felt herself blush. "Not exactly. I rented a horse and I suppose there was a reason his fee was so cheap. He threw me off earlier this afternoon and ran away, probably back to Fort William. If I start walking back tomorrow morning, I should return by the middle of the afternoon."

Calum shook his head. "Nonsense."

Louise's earlier feelings of warmth and attraction evaporated a little. Some of her fear returned. "I beg your pardon?"

He stumbled over his next words. "I could take you back in my ornithopter. Well, it isn't mine, but I have leave to use it. I have enough fuel for the journey to Fort William and back to the barony."

"Barony?"

"Roseheath is a barony," he explained. "I live on the estate. I have for my whole life. I'm here on an errand for the baron."

Louise was unfamiliar with the workings of the aristocracy, but being sent to a mountainside by a baron seemed a trifle strange. "What sort of errand?"

He pointed at the river. "Collecting some water for one of his experiments. Lord MacAulay is an inventor. He invented these candles, in fact." He held up the flameless candle, one of what had to be thousands used across Great Britain.

That piece of information wasn't what struck Louise, though. It was his appearance—his nose growing a little longer, lips thinning, chin slightly pointier. It must be the candlelight playing tricks on her eyes. It was nearly dark.

But there was something else she noticed, something she would want pointed out if it happened to her. "You're drooling," she said.

Calum touched his lips. "Damn it." Before she could offer a rejoinder, he looked up at the sky, a panicked look on his face. "It's too late for me to sail the skies again tonight." He seemed to be speaking to himself, rather than her. Turning to Louise, he said, "Tonight, stay in your tent and don't come out."

"That seems the smart thing to do in the wilderness." Despite her flip remark, her heartbeat picked up speed, thumping against her ribs so hard she was sure he must be able to hear it.

His expression softened. "It wasn't my intention to frighten you. Yes, it's prudent to stay in a tent during the night." He cleared his throat and looked away. "Especially during the full moon. I thought it wasn't for another night or so."

Louise hadn't thought the conversation could take on a stranger note, but it seemed to have done so. The only response she could think of was, "At least there will be light."

"Yes." He sighed heavily. "Go on to your tent, Louise. I'll keep watch for things that go bump in the night."

She collected her sketchbook with her uninjured hand. She *was* tired and sore—being thrown from a horse would do that to a person. In retrospect, she should be grateful that her worst injury was a sprained wrist. "Good night."

In the flicker of the flameless candle's light, Calum replied, "Good night, Louise."

The almanac had been wrong about the full moon. It was nearly here, calling to Calum's inner wolf, would make its appearance very soon judging by the way his muscles contracted and ached, fighting to shift. The moon was bad enough to think about; how he would have to shift away from his pack, in open sight of a human woman only a few yards away. What was worse was his wolf was screaming at him that Louise Bell was his mate. It had started nagging at him as soon as she came into view while he piloted the ornithopter, then protested in rage when Calum offered to bring her back to Fort William.

Take her back to Roseheath. She's your mate. You don't have to ask. She's yours.

Shut up, he told it as sternly as he could. *She has agency. We don't steal brides in Scotland anymore, werewolf or not.*

After Louise had retreated to her tent, Calum waited a half hour to ensure she wouldn't come back out. He left his clothes in the ornithopter's flight basket, padding on bare feet to a copse of trees not too far from where she had set it up. His logical, human part pointed out that there wasn't enough distance, warring with his primal, animalistic side that reminded him that she was going to have to learn about shifters sooner or later.

And damn himself if he didn't know which part of himself he should listen to.

He settled among the trees, thinking about the sleeping woman only yards away. Louise was perfect. Her dark hair was held off her face in a long braid that hung down her back, wisps escaping it to frame her heart-shaped face. Her green eyes were bright, framed by dark lashes, cheeks pink against a suntanned face. She wore sensible brown trousers that were a little too large for her frame but still showed off ample curves he already wanted to touch. His body tightened as lascivious images ran through his mind, making his breath hitch.

Is it Louise, or am I starting to shift? He couldn't see the moon from his vantage point, but could feel its presence. His limbs started to lengthen, nose growing into a snout. Fur sprouted along his body.

Shifting it is!

He'd been shifting since he was five, twenty-one years ago now, and it was still painful every time. Calum gritted his teeth throughout the change, knowing that fighting it would only prolong the pain, until he rested on four paws, the feel of the earth beneath him reassuring in its solidity. He sniffed the ground, delighted and curious with the new smells around him, until he remembered that there was a human nearby. Calum couldn't howl as he wanted to.

The scent of water from the river was unmistakable, different from the water at Roseheath. *I suppose the baron was correct about different water.* Belatedly, he realized he still hadn't collected water. *I'll remember in the morning.*

He walked out of the copse, ignoring every impulse to run, especially when he picked up the scent of a deer. A low growl of frustration escaped him when he remembered that he couldn't hunt tonight, couldn't bay to the moon that commanded he shift. Glancing at the tent, he reminded himself that it would be worth the effort.

Would it be inappropriate to ask the baron how he broke the news about his being a werewolf to the baroness? Theirs had been an arranged marriage, the baroness being human and unaware of the existence of shifters until after she arrived in Roseheath. Calum's mother was descended from wolves, although she couldn't shift herself. Who the hell did he know who could help him figure out what to do when one's mate sent by the gods was a human?

The rustle of fabric had him out of his ruminations, heart pounding. Without looking over, he already knew what he would see if he turned his head: Louise at the ornithopter, holding his clothes and wondering where the hell he was.

God damn it.

When he looked at the ornithopter, he saw his predictions were correct. Louise, still wearing her trousers and blouse, held up his clothing, only dropping it when she saw him.

Louise had never seen a wolf in her life, but she suspected that they had to be smaller than the furry creature staring at her, frozen in place on four gigantic paws. Cautiously, she reached out and closed the ornithopter's flight basket door, an irrational part of her convinced that a waist-high piece of wood would keep her safe from a wild animal that wasn't otherwise found in Scotland.

Had the wolf attacked Calum? No, she quickly decided. His clothes wouldn't have been folded in a neat pile on the basket floor. She'd come out here to talk to him, curiosity winning out over the words of warning he'd left her with before she returned to her tent. Curiosity, and no small amount of attraction. She'd been horrified to find him gone.

The wolf took a few careful steps toward her. Louise didn't move, hardly daring to breathe, as she surveyed the flight basket's interior. There was a lever to activate the ornithopter's wings, or was that the engine? Even in the bright silver light offered by the moon overhead, she couldn't read the words printed on the brass plaques that identified the instruments, held in place by copper nails along the basket's rails. Letting out a cry of frustration and fear, she leaned against the back of the basket.

The wolf closed the distance between them, sitting on its haunches as it stared at her with big golden eyes. *They look like Calum's.*

She looked at the clothing, then back at the wolf. An insane idea struck her, and beneath it, a strange surety that the creature before her was him. Clearing her throat, she whispered, "Calum?"

The animal nodded, his head bobbing awkwardly. He placed a paw on the edge of the basket.

"Oh, my God." Some of her fear ebbed away. "You're not going to hurt me or eat me, are you?"

The wolf chuffed and shook his head, like the very idea was repugnant.

"Can you turn back into a human?"

Another nod.

"Now?"

He shook his head again, then removed his paw from the basket's edge. He raised his head at the moon, stomping one of his paws, as if in frustration. Perhaps he was compelled to stay in this form for the night.

Louise opened the basket door and stepped out, approaching him. "Can I pet you?"

Calum shoved his head under her hand. His dense, dark fur was shaggy, probably the same dark color as his hair, if the moonlight was anything to go by. He nuzzled her fingers with his long snout.

"Will you tell me what's going on in the morning?" she asked.

He chuffed again, then nodded.

∼

The sun was peeking over the mountainside when Calum shifted back into his human form. Through the open tent flap, he could see the top of Louise's head. His heart swelled with affection for her, a deep need to take her home with him.

Her deep, even breaths told him that she was still sleeping. That might make things a little less awkward after they had their chat.

Calum quickly dressed, then returned to the tent. His stomach growled, reminding him that he hadn't had the chance to hunt rabbits last night. Ignoring his hunger, he returned to the tent as Louise lifted her head. She hauled herself up to a seated position with her good hand, still staying in the tent. He sat across from her on the hard ground. "You're a wolf." Her voice was blunt. Calum appreciated that.

"Yes."

"And you can do that whenever you want?"

"No, only during the full moon. Some wolves can shift at will, but I'm not one of them. Our pack's leader does."

She raised a dark eyebrow. "You have a pack?"

"Of course. Wolves often live in packs. It's part of our nature." He cleared his throat, unsure how to go about this next part. He may as well be as blunt as she was. "I think you're my mate."

Her eyes widened in surprise. "How?"

"It's something wolves talk about but don't often experience. I think it's the reason I was compelled to stop here yesterday. Something in me recognized that."

She didn't reply immediately. She didn't run away either, which Calum had to take as a good sign.

Louise's next words were slow, deliberate. "When you said that you recognized me somewhere…"

"It was my wolf, seeing his mate."

"All right, although that sounds insane." Something in Calum deflated. "But so is seeing a real werewolf," she continued.

Hope flared in him.

"There's something I recognized in you, too," she added. "Like we were supposed to meet. I can't explain it." She glanced over his shoulder for a few seconds, giving herself time to collect her thoughts, he guessed. "I like you a lot."

"Oh, thank God," he said. "And I like you, too."

"What happens next?" she asked.

"Do you want to see Roseheath?" he asked.

"Do I have to stay there? Can I go back to Bowhill?"

"Of course, you don't. You're welcome to leave whenever you wish. I can't, though."

"Why not?"

"The Roseheath pack has a long-standing royal decree we must abide by. Wolves can't leave Scotland."

Her fingers flew to her mouth in shock. "The *Queen* knows of you?"

"The Queen wasn't the one who forced the agreement, but I assume she does."

"No!"

He nodded. "Yes. You're free to travel. I am not."

"Would you make me like you?" she asked.

"No. Wolves are born, not made." Their children were likely to have some shifting ability, should they have any, but he supposed it might be too early to start discussing a family.

She looked at him thoughtfully for a long moment before speaking. "All right."

His heart leapt against his chest. "All right, you'll come back to Roseheath with me?"

"Yes, I'd like to see it. There might be something good to draw there."

He rose, then helped her to her feet without being prompted. *Mine, mine, mine,* his wolf happily brayed inside him. "I have a nice little house," he said. "My mother's isn't too far away. She'll be delighted to meet you. I think the whole pack will be, actually. It's so rare to meet your true mate."

Louise didn't let go of him immediately, keeping her hands tucked in his. The feel of her bandaged arm reminded him of her injury, how he'd thoughtlessly forgotten it. "How is your wrist this morning?"

"I've hardly noticed the pain."

"I'll still help you pack, either way." He reluctantly let her go, then surveyed the tent. He'd never taken one down in his life.

Louise sighed, then gave him a smile that made his toes curl. "I'll show you what to do."

Louise adjusted the goggles over her eyes, then gripped the side of the flight basket as the ornithopter's wings began to beat against the air, fighting gravity. She'd flown on dirigibles before, but nothing as small and open as the craft she found herself in now. Surprisingly, she didn't feel nauseated as she looked over the basket at the ground. Beneath them, Ben Nevis looked absolutely spectacular, the river flowing between trees at its shores.

She waited to speak until they were fully airborne. Calum visibly relaxed, his hands loosening around the controls. She pulled down her goggles so she could see him better, blinking against the breeze over the treetops. "Calum."

He turned to face her, removing his own goggles. "Yes? Is everything all right? Are you feeling sick?"

"I'm fine," she said. "As fine as one can be when one has just found out they have a mate." Her palms were sweating, and she rubbed them against the rough linen of her trousers. "Actually, I wanted to do something." Taking a deep breath, she leaned up to him, pressing a kiss to his lips.

His response was immediate. With a groan, he kissed her back, hands wrapping around her hips. Both of their breaths came fast, and a ripple of desire coursed through her at the thought of doing that again. "Louise," he murmured.

She rested her head against his chest. "Mm?"

There was a smile in his voice when he replied. "I forgot to bring back the water."

Louise couldn't help it. Dissolving into giggles, she squeezed his hand and looked ahead, at the mountainous landscape to an unexpected future.

ABOUT THE AUTHOR

Jessica Marting is a sci-fi and paranormal romance author, art enthusiast (not quite an artist, despite all that time in art school), an avid reader, and makeup collector. She lives in Toronto.

For updates about books, giveaways, and other fun stuff, subscribe to her newsletter: jessicamarting.com/news letter

Magic & Mechanicals

Wolf's Lady

Sea Change

Bound in Blood

Dragon's Keep

Spellbound

Afterlife

Queen of Feathers

The Searchers

Blood Ties

Blood Moon

Blood Virtue

Zone Cyborgs

Haven

Paradise

Oasis

Safe Harbor

Sanctuary

Refuge

The Commons

Supernova

Celestial Chaos

New Eden

Contact

Bonded

Recharge

Echo

Standalone Novels & Novellas

Spindle's End

Trade Secrets

Neon Vice

Dead Ringer

Escape From Europa 10

Castaways

Demon's Favor

Rapture

Her Purrfect Match